DOCTOR WHO
HORNS OF NIMON

DOCTOR WHO
AND THE
HORNS OF NIMON

Based on the BBC television serial by Anthony Read by
arrangement with the British Broadcasting Corporation

TERRANCE DICKS

No. 31 in the Doctor Who Library

A TARGET BOOK
published by
the paperback division of
W. H. ALLEN & Co. Ltd

A Target Book
Published in 1980
by the Paperback Division of W. H. Allen & Co. Ltd.
A Howard & Wyndham Company
44 Hill Street, London W1X 8LB

Reprinted 1982
Reprinted 1984

Novelisation copyright © Terrance Dicks 1980
Original script copyright © Anthony Read 1979
'Doctor Who' series copyright © British Broadcasting
Corporation 1979, 1980

Printed and bound in Great Britain by
Anchor Brendon Ltd, Tiptree, Essex

ISBN 0 426 20131 0

Contents

Prologue

The Coming of the Nimon

Next to the crumbling Palace of the Emperor, on the edge of the sprawling ruins that were the capital of Skonnos, there rose the Power Complex. It was a gleaming, metallic, star-shaped edifice, dominated by the two enormous horns that rose from its central unit. All around, mile upon mile of ruined and half-ruined buildings bore silent witness to the end of a once-great star empire.

No enemy had ever defeated the Skonnons. They destroyed themselves. An aggressive race, with a talent for war and conquest, they had discovered high technology and space flight much earlier than their neighbouring planets. Armed with superior weaponry they had swept over the galaxy in an expanding wave of conquest. In an astonishingly short time they were the masters of a hundred worlds, the famous First Skonnan Empire.

The aggressive streak that had brought them success was to cause their downfall. The noble families fell to fighting amongst themselves, Emperor followed Emperor in quick succession, rival Emperors set up against each other, and soon the Skonnan Empire, like ancient Rome before it, collapsed from within.

Planet after planet took advantage of the confusion to throw off the Skonnan yoke, the occupying armies retreated, and the last devastating civil war was fought on Skonnos itself. It left the planet in ruins. When the fighting ended, a handful of well-protected senior officers commanding a few squads of Skonnan troops were the sole survivors in a shattered capital, victors in a civil war that had ended through sheer exhaustion.

Then came the Nimon.

One day a mysterious silver sphere appeared, just outside the Palace. General Sato, Commander of the few remaining Skonnan troops, routed out Soldeed, a middle-aged laboratory technician, and sent him to investigate. Soldeed protested that he was no scientist. Sato pointed out that he was the nearest they'd got, and drove him out to the capsule at blaster point.

Long hours later, Soldeed returned, swollen with new self-importance, and carrying a metal staff ending in two strange horn-like prongs. The sphere, he said, was the abode of a god-like being called the Nimon, who had come to offer help to the people of Skonnos. Provided that the proper conditions were met, the Nimon was prepared to offer nothing less than the restoration of the Skonnan Empire. Soldeed was to be the voice of the Nimon from now on.

Sato scoffed and demanded to see the Nimon for himself. Soldeed pointed the staff at him, a ray shot from the horns, and Sato fell dead. Captain Sorak, Sato's aide-de-camp, became a prompt convert to the Nimon's cause. So did the rest of the officers and their men.

Under Soldeed's orders, work began. First the Power Complex was constructed, swallowing up the original sphere which lay concealed somewhere at its centre. A spaceship was found, and patched up into working order with the help of certain new equipment provided by the Nimon. Finally all was ready and the spaceship was despatched on the Nimon's business.

For the Nimon demanded tribute—tribute and

sacrifice. Seven times the sacrifice was to be made. Seven youths and maidens of high birth were to be provided on each occasion, each carrying a crystal of Hymetusite, the most radioactive substance in the galaxy.

Neither sacrifice nor tribute was available on Skonnos, but fortunately the planet Aneth was their nearest neighbour. The Anethans were a peace-loving people, and their planet had suffered far less than Skonnos itself in the Empire wars. But when the black Skonnan battle cruiser appeared in their skies, the memory of past defeats paralysed the Anethans with terror.

Meekly they handed over the sacrifices and tribute, as demanded. Six times already the sacrifice had taken place. The terrified young Anethans had been brought to Skonnos as captives. Holding lead caskets of Hymetusite, they had been driven into the Power Complex, never to be seen again.

Now the return of the battle cruiser with the seventh and final sacrifice was eagerly awaited on Skonnos.

But the seventh sacrifice failed to arrive on time.

1

Ship of Sacrifice

The spaceship was old.

It was a Skonnan battle cruiser, massive, black, threatening, sole survivor of a fleet that had once dominated the galaxy. As it lumbered towards its home planet, Skonnos, gun-ports bristling with space-cannon, it was still a terrifying sight—but the ship was old, almost obsolete.

Drive systems were erratic, navigational circuits unreliable, main computers on overload, the automatic pilot at break-down point. Few of the laser-cannon would still fire and those that did were as likely to blow up the ship as destroy the enemy.

In the main control room, the crew laboured worriedly at the failing controls. There were two of them, black-uniformed, and red-helmeted in typical Skonnan style. Sekkoth, the Captain, was a wizened, grey-haired veteran of the First Empire. Sardor, his co-pilot, was a younger man, plump-faced and overweight. He had been too young to serve in the First Empire Wars and, perhaps as a result, he was even more fiercely militaristic than his superior.

The ship was operating on minimum power and the gloomy control room was cluttered with a hodge-podge of obsolete equipment, festooned with trailing cables and dangling power leads.

Sardor studied the faint, erratic display on the read-out screen of an antiquated computer. 'Seems to be malfunctioning again. Still, not long to go now.'

Captain Sekkoth looked up from the feebly flickering instrument dials. 'You've been overloading it,' he said pettishly. 'I warned you what would happen, my instructions were quite clear, all subsidiary functions have to be rerouted through the back-up computer.'

'But that takes hours!'

Sekkoth shrugged. 'We're only twelve hours out from Aneth. It'll be at least another twelve back to Skonnos.'

Grunting, Sardor straightened up. 'It'd be a lot less if this ship was working properly. When are we going to get these new ships they keep promising. When are we going to *fight*?'

'Soon—when the Nimon fulfills his promise. Be patient.'

'Patience?' snarled Sardor. 'Patience is for the weak. Skonnans were made to fight, to conquer, to rule—as we did in the days when this ship was built. You remember, Sekkoth, you were there.'

The older man smiled. 'You'll get all the fighting you want soon. The Nimon will give us new weapons, we'll reconquer the galaxy—'

'*When?*'

'When we have fulfilled our part of the bargain.'

'And when will that be?'

Sekkoth paused impressively. 'Perhaps I shouldn't tell you this, but this is the last shipment! Once it is delivered, our side of the contract will be fulfilled. Now do you see the importance of our mission?'

Sardor stared at him, unable to believe that the military glory he lusted for was so close. '*This* cargo is the last one?'

'Yes.'

'I'd better go and check that it's safe,' Sardor hurried

from the control room.

He made his way along grey metal corridors to a heavy door in which was set a small window. Sardor peered through the window, studying the half-dozen figures huddled together in the hold. Three youths and four maidens, all wearing the short golden robes of Anethan nobility. 'Weakling scum,' growled Sardor. Turning away in disgust he hurried back to the control room.

Sekkoth looked up. 'Well? How are they?'

'Same as always—inferior, craven beings, just like all Anethans.' Sardor laughed. 'We turn up in an old ship like this, and the Anethans meekly surrender the cream of their aristocracy—not to mention their most valuable minerals.'

Sekkoth smiled grimly. 'The Anethans still remember when these were the most feared ships in the skies. We devastated their planet, taught them to fear and obey us. That was in the old days, before we started fighting amongst ourselves.'

Sekkoth's news had filled Sardor with impatience. 'It doesn't have to take us twelve hours to reach Skonnos, you know. We can do it in nine hours, maybe six, if we use the overdrive.'

'And suppose we overload it?'

'What does it matter? Once we get back to Skonnons with this last cargo, this ship will never have to fly again.' Sardor tapped out a projection on the navigational computer. 'You see, no problem at all. We can do it in six hours easily.'

Before Sekkoth could stop him he reached out and threw the overdrive lever. There was a sudden roar of power—and an instrument console exploded in a shower of sparks.

'You blundering idiot!' shouted Sekkoth. 'You've overloaded it. The automatic pilot's blown.'

13

Whitefaced, Sardor hurried to another console. 'It'll be all right, won't it?'

'Will it? We're off-course already.'

'We can fly her on manual,' babbled Sardor. 'All we have to do is find the beacon.' He fumbled with controls and a moment later a steady beeping filled the control room. Sardor smiled with relief. 'There's the beacon, we can home in on the signal.'

Suddenly the beep began to fade. 'We're losing it! I'll alter course and push the engines to full power.' The engines screamed louder, and the whole cabin began to vibrate. Still the beep grew fainter.

'You hot-headed idiot,' yelled Sekkoth. 'Now the whole ship's going out of control!' He began wrestling with the controls. 'Steer, blast you, steer!'

'Something's pulling us back,' shouted Sardor. 'It's too strong for us, there's nothing I can do . . .'

A sudden terrific explosion ripped out part of the console; Sekkoth staggered and fell dead over his controls.

The beacon faded and vanished completely, as some mysterious force drew the ship ever closer . . .

In the cargo hold the young captives clung together as the old spaceship rattled and shook. A slender fair-haired girl called Teka turned to the sturdy brown-haired boy at her side. 'What's happening, Seth?'

'I've no idea.' He put his arm around her, drawing her closer.

She looked up at him confidently. 'You'll look after me, won't you?'

The ship was shaking itself to pieces and soon they would all be dead, he thought. But he smiled down at her and said confidently, 'Yes, of course I will.'

Around them their fellow captives were sobbing with

fear, but Teka was unafraid. Seth would look after her.

Seth was a hero.

Not far away another kind of ship hung suspended in space. From the outside it looked like a police box of a kind once used on a planet called Earth. In reality, it was a space/time craft called the TARDIS, with the remarkable property of being bigger on the inside then on the outside.

However, the TARDIS did have one thing in common with the Skonnan battle cruiser. For a ship of its kind it was old-fashioned, not to say obsolete, and its inner workings often gave its owner trouble.

They were doing so at this very moment. The central column of the many-sided control console was partially dismantled and the ship's owner was staring at it in mild concern. The owner of this particular ship was a rebel Time Lord, a mysterious traveller in space and time known only as the Doctor. He was a tall, wide-eyed, curly-haired man dressed in a loose assortment of comfortable, vaguely Bohemian-looking clothing. A broad-brimmed soft hat and an incredibly long scarf hung on a hat stand nearby.

'Well, that should immobilise her for the moment,' said the Doctor thankfully.

He picked up a crumpled owner's manual and leafed through it.

From somewhere near floor-level an electronic voice said, 'Correction, Master, The TARDIS is moving.'

The Doctor looked down. At his feet was a kind of robot dog. This was K9, a mobile self-powered computer, the Doctor's valued, if sometimes irritating, companion.

Ignoring him, the Doctor studied the manual. 'When making modifications, it is important to shut down everything, except that which it is not necessary to shut down.' He looked up from the book. 'You see K9? Terribly easy to damage something important otherwise.' The Doctor adjusted a circuit, there was a spatter of blue sparks and he snatched his hand away. 'Like me, for instance!' He made a quick adjustment with his sonic screwdriver. 'Better disconnect that one too. Now she should hold steady.'

'I repeat, Master, the TARDIS is still moving.'

'Nonsense, K9, I've just immobilised her, haven't I?'

'Affirmative.'

'Well, then?'

'The TARDIS is still moving. Accelerating fast.'

'What? How can we be?'

A small pretty girl with long fair hair came into the control room. She wore a red jacket, white trousers and a ruffled shirt. This was Romana, the Doctor's Time Lady companion.

The Doctor was just about to enquire why she found it necessary to imitate the traditional dress of the fox-hunters of planet Earth, when Romana distracted him. 'K9's right, you know, Doctor!'

'What? How can he be right when he's just disagreed with me?'

She went over to the other side of the console and studied a row of flickering dials. 'The TARDIS seems to disagree with you as well. Look!'

The Doctor came to look. 'We do seem to be moving, don't we?'

'Yes. And very fast.'

The Doctor said. 'But the power's off. *Everything's* off—except what's on,' he added, sucking his finger.

'Everything? What have you been doing?'

'Oh, just trying out an idea I had. A slight modification to the conceptual geometer.'

'Doctor, this is a very old ship. She just can't take all

this tinkering any more. It could be dangerous.'

'Nonsense, I know what I'm doing. Nothing could possibly go—'

The TARDIS gave a sudden violent lurch and the Doctor clutched at the console to steady himself. 'You know , I really must stop saying that. Every time I say nothing can go wrong, something always goes—' the TARDIS lurched again '—wrong!' concluded the Doctor. 'Uncanny, isn't it?'

Romana was still checking instrument readings. 'We're being *pulled*, Doctor. Some kind of gravitational field.'

'My dear Romana, do you really think I'd dismantle half the control system, including the conceptual geometer *and* the dematerialisation circuits if there was the slightest risk of—'

Romana gave a gasp of horror. 'You've dismantled the dematerialisation circuits?'

The Doctor touched a control and the cover of the scanner screen slid back. 'Let's take a look outside.'

The scanner's screen was filled with swirling darkness. 'There you are,' said the Doctor triumphantly. 'Nothing there but blackness.'

'*Moving* blackness,' corrected Romana. 'And it's moving very fast. Or rather we're moving very fast.'

The Doctor looked thoughtfully at the screen. 'You know what, Romana? I think we're moving—very fast!'

A terrifying thought came into Romana's mind. 'Maybe we're falling into a black hole?'

'No, that whatever-it-is isn't pulling hard enough for that. Anyway a black hole would have been on the TARDIS charts—unless it's a new one, of course.'

'I hope you're right. Thanks to you, we can't dematerialise and get away from here. And if we do get sucked into a black hole . . .'

The Doctor's face lit up. As always, he seemed

17

positively to enjoy the prospect of danger. 'Fascinating, isn't it? I wonder what it would feel like?'

'Well, don't stand there wondering about it. Do something. Put the TARDIS together again!'

'All right, all right,' muttered the Doctor irritably, and set to work on the dismantled central column. 'Come and give me a paw, will you, K9?'

As K9 glided forward, there was a blinding flash followed by a tremendous bang. Clouds of smoke poured from the control column. The shock sent K9 shooting backwards across the control room to crash into the opposite wall.

Still coughing, the Doctor went over to K9. 'Are you all right?'

K9 didn't reply—which was hardly surprising, since his head appeared to be on backwards.

Carefully the Doctor took hold of K9's head and turned it the right way round. 'Are you all right, K9?'

'Affirmative, Master.'

Romana fanned away the smoke. 'What was all that about?'

'Don't worry. It was only the defense shields blowing.'

'*Only*—Can you fix them again?'

'Of course I can—given time.'

Romana looked at the scanner screen. 'Time is just what we don't have, Doctor.'

There was something on the screen, a tiny point that grew larger and larger as it sped nearer.

'Fascinating! Do you know Romana, I think it's a spaceship!'

The shape grew larger and larger, until they could make out the lines of an ancient battered-looking battle cruiser.

'It is a spaceship,' said Romana grimly. 'And we're heading straight towards it—on a collision course!'

2

The Skonnons

It was a dark and stormy day on Skonnos, black clouds
swirling beneath grey skies.

Captain Sorak was inspecting the guards outside the
Power Complex, waiting for Soldeed to return from one
of his conferences with the Nimon. Like his men, Sorak
wore the black Skonnan uniform with the addition of the
horned helmet that symbolised their service to the
Nimon.

The elaborately ornamented gateway to the Complex
was shielded by a forcefield. No-one but Soldeed and
Anethan Sacrifice had ever been through that shimmering red barrier—and only Soldeed had ever come out
again.

Sorak noticed a shuddering of the forcefield and
seconds later Soldeed stepped through and stood survey-
ing them imperiously.

He was a very different figure from the terrified
technician who had first made contact with the Nimon.
Now Soldeed wore a gorgeous black cloak with the high
collar of the Skonnan aristocracy. He had cultivated a
flowing moustache and a pointed beard in an effort to
add authority to his otherwise undistinguished features.
For audiences with the Nimon he wore a golden circlet
with a great jewel blazing at its centre.

All in all, thought Sorak, Soldeed was getting con-

19

siderably above himself. Once the Nimon had delivered the promised technology, Soldeed would have to go. Meanwhile he must be endured. In fact, since he alone had the ear of the Nimon, he must be flattered and courted.

The guards crashed to attention, Sorak saluted, and Soldeed stood savouring the moment.

After a suitably impressive pause, he said sonorously, 'I have spoken with the Nimon.'

'And what does he say, Soldeed?'

Soldeed frowned, not caring for the younger man's tone. 'He says many things, Sorak, many things.' The implication was clear—the substance of Soldeed's conversations with the Nimon was too high for common minds to grasp. 'He speaks of the Great Journey of Life. He speaks of conquest. He speaks of the Great Skonnos, rising from its own ashes with wings of flame.'

Sorak said drily. 'Does he speak of the new ships he promised us?'

'He does, Sorak, he does. He says we shall have them, and soon. All he demands is the seventh and final sacrifice from Aneth.'

Sceptical as he was, Sorak desperately wanted to believe what Soldeed was saying. 'Then he really will keep his promises to us? There will be new ships, new weapons?'

'There will, Sorak, there will. The *Second* Skonnan Empire is about to be born.'

The Doctor looked up from the central column, shaking his head. 'It's no good, I'll never do it in time.'

Romana looked at the scanner, now totally filled with the black hulk of the alien ship. 'So we're just going to crash straight into that—with no defence shields?'

'Collision imminent, Master,' confirmed K9.

With a clangorous thud the TARDIS struck. The impact threw the Doctor and Romana to the floor, and jarred a few more bits loose from the dismantled column.

The Doctor picked himself up and helped Romana to her feet. 'Quite right, K9,' he said cheerfully, 'we seem to have arrived.' He looked at the scanner, which showed a vista of corroded metal hull. 'We must be jammed right up against the side of the ship. Pretty battered old thing, may have been here for years, centuries even. Let's go and take a look at it, shall we?'

Romana sighed. Something told her that Doctor's insatiable curiosity was about to lead them into new dangers. 'How are we going to get on board?'

'The defence shield on the door operates on a separate circuit. If I can reactivate it and extrude it . . .'

'If you can *what*?'

The Doctor worked busily for a few moments and then said proudly, 'Look!' He touched a control and the TARDIS door slid open.

Beyond the door was a kind of transparent energy-corridor, leading directly to the airlock of the other ship. 'There,' said the Doctor proudly. 'What do you think of that?'

'Well done, Doctor!'

'Oh, it was nothing really,' said the Doctor modestly. 'Merely a completely unparalleled scientific achievement. Come on.' Grabbing hat and scarf, the Doctor stepped into the energy-corridor. K9 glided after him and Romana followed.

It felt rather eerie to be standing in mid-space, but a few minutes work with the Doctor's sonic screwdriver opened the airlock and soon they were inside the alien ship.

Romana looked around, wondering if it had been worth the effort. They were in a gloomy metal hold

21

which seemed to contain nothing but a row of seven lead caskets lined up against the wall.

Curious as ever, the Doctor went over and opened the nearest, revealing a chunk of glowing crystal in a lead-lined container. Romana said curiously, 'That's Hymetusite, isn't it?'

'I do believe it is.'

'Isn't Hymetusite highly radioactive?'

'Yes, it is. I wonder what it's doing here . . . '

There was a sudden ticking from K9. 'Danger, Master. I detect ultra-radiation emissions, level Q 7.325.'

Hastily the Doctor closed the lid of the casket and put it back. 'Thank you, K9. And now?'

'Level falling . . . now Q 1.861 and still falling.'

'Good. Listen, K9, we're going to explore this ship, see what makes things tick around here.'

'Ticking caused by radiation, Master. Radiation source probably crystal of Hymetusite.'

'Not that sort of ticking!'

'Master?'

'Oh, never mind. I want you to go back to the TARDIS control room and do a full systems check. Inspect all circuits so I'll know exactly what I've got to put right.'

'Affirmative, Master.'

'Off you go then!' K9 glided away.

Romana meanwhile was exploring the rest of the hold. 'There's another door over here, but it seems to be locked . . . I suppose this ship must have been converted to some kind of freighter?'

'Not a passenger vessel, anyway. No-one in their right mind would carry Hymetusite and passengers.'

'I wonder where it was heading?'

'Who knows?' said the Doctor vaguely. He wandered over to Romana and tried the door. 'It's locked!'

'I just told you that.'

The Doctor produced his sonic screwdriver and in a few minutes the door was open. 'After you, Romana.'

'After *you*, Doctor!'

The Doctor stepped through the door.

He found himself in another hold much like the first. It contained a group of young people, three young men and four girls, in short golden robes.

The Doctor nodded affably. 'Hello, what are you doing here.'

The little group cowered away in terror.

The Doctor fished a crumpled paper bag from his pocket. 'Here, have a jelly baby?' He held out the bag, and the young man in front of the group leaped back. 'It's all right, they're quite harmless,' said the Doctor reassuringly. He popped one in his mouth and said indistinctly, 'See? Here, show them, Romana.' Obediently Romana took a jelly baby.

The Doctor held the bag out. 'Help yourself!'

Hesitantly the young man took a sweet, and somehow the ridiculous little ritual seemed to calm them. 'Who are you?'

'I'm the Doctor and this is Romana. Who are you?'

Before the young man could answer, a fair-haired girl next to him said proudly, 'His name's Seth. He's a prince from Aneth. I am Princess Teka.'

'So you come from Aneth? Delightful planet.'

'You've been there?'

'Well, yes, but not yet, if you see what I mean.

It was clear that she didn't. 'Do you know where we are?'

'Nowhere,' said Romana briefly. 'Where are you going?'

'To Skonnos. We are the bearers of Aneth's tribute to the Nimon.'

The Doctor stared at them. 'What?'

23

'We are the bearers of Aneth's tribute to the Nimon.'

'All right, all right, I heard you the first time. What a very curious thing to be.'

'We were on our way to Skonnos when something went wrong with the ship. It seemed to go out of control. I heard an explosion and, well, here we are!'

'Here, as you so rightly say, we are,' agreed the Doctor.

There was a muffled clang, then a series of other smaller ones.

Seth looked alarmed. 'What was that?'

'Sounds like meteorites hitting the ship, wouldn't you say, Romana?'

Romana nodded. 'We must be in some kind of gravity whirlpool.'

'Trapped in a Sargasso Sea in space . . . ! Romana, suppose someone was trying to create a black hole, artificially?'

'Can it be done?'

'Oh yes—all you need is a focussed gravity beam. Attract matter to one point in space and when there was enough concentration it'd start to collapse with its own weight.'

'But why would anyone want to do such a thing—' Romana broke off. 'Is it my imagination, or is the gravity in here increasing?'

The Doctor gave a little jump. 'I think you're right. Unless we can get this ship away from here, we're going to be crushed to a singularity.'

'What's happening?' demanded Seth. 'What's a singularity?'

'A mathematical point with no dimensions . . .'

Seth stared at him, none the wiser.

'Never mind, Seth. Tell me who's in command of this ship?'

A voice said, 'I am.'

The Doctor turned and saw that a door on the other side of the hold had opened. In it stood a black-uniformed figure, covering him with a double-barrelled blaster.

3

Sardor in Command

'How do you do?' said the Doctor with his usual friendliness. 'I'm very glad to meet you, whoever you are.'

'I'm Sardor, acting Captain of this Skonnan battle cruiser.'

'Well, I'm the Doctor and this is Romana, and—'

'What are you doing with the sacrifices?'

'Are you telling me these young people are to be sacrificed?'

'They are sacrifices to the Nimon. And who are you?' Before the Doctor could speak, Sardor answered his own question. 'You're space pirates, aren't you, come to steal the Hymetusite?'

'Certainly not. We came to see if anyone needed help.'

'Why should I believe you?'

'That's a very good question! Now here's one for you. This entire ship is heading into deadly danger. Do you know how to get it away from here?'

'Do you?'

'I might.'

'What are you—a pilot? A scientist? An engineer?'

'Yes!' said the Doctor comprehensively. 'Now why don't you put that thing away and show me your control room?'

Sardor considered for a moment and then stepped

aside, motioning the Doctor towards the door with his blaster. 'This way.'

'You're not going to put that thing away?'

'I said this way! And get your hands up.'

'All right, if that's the way you want to play it.' The Doctor raised his hands. 'Though how I'm going to repair your ship like this . . .'

'Move—both of you!'

They moved.

With a final glare at the Anethans, Sardor followed them through the door.

He herded the Doctor and Romana through the gloomy corridors of the ship to the cluttered control room.

The Doctor looked down at the dead body in the pilot's seat. 'Who's that?'

'Captain Sekkoth. He was killed when the console blew up.'

'How very unfortunate!'

'It could have been a lot worse. At least the cargo is still safe.'

'You mean the Hymetusite?' asked Romana.

'That, and the sacrifices.'

'What sacrifices?' demanded the Doctor.

'The Anethans—you saw them. I have to get them safely to Skonnos whatever happens. They are to be sacrificed to the Nimon as the final payment in our Great Contract.'

'I don't think I like the sound of that.'

Sardor jabbed him in the ribs with the blaster. 'It doesn't matter what you like, Doctor. Now get to work!'

Soldeed sat brooding in his laboratory. It was a large room filled with complicated pieces of electronic equipment, whose working was a complete and utter mystery

28

to him. To maintain his status as a great scientist, Soldeed had taken over a room in the Palace and filled it with all the scientific equipment that could be salvaged from the ruins of the city.

Now the room was a jumble of gadgetry, most of it damaged beyond repair. Soldeed spent hours in the laboratory tinkering away, hoping desperately to get something—anything—working again.

With a sigh, he abandoned the piece of machinery he was tinkering with and stared out of the window at the angular metallic shape of the Power Complex, dominated by the huge metal horns that jutted up into the grey skies of Skonnos. In his heart Soldeed knew he was no scientist. He was merely bluffing, keeping up appearances until the Nimon gave him the scientific knowledge and equipment that would confirm his power.

He heard someone coming, and bent hastily over his work.

Sorak marched into the room. 'I have news, Soldeed.'

For a moment Soldeed pretended to be too absorbed to notice him. 'What is it, Sorak? I have important work to do.'

Sorak looked round the junk-cluttered room. 'Forgive me for interrupting your—scientific labours, but this is important.'

'Well?'

'I don't really know how to tell you, but—'

'Why not begin at the beginning, and continue to the end?'

'It's the battle cruiser from Aneth, sir, the ship bringing the final sacrifices.'

'What about it?'

'It hasn't arrived—it seems to have disappeared!'

Soldeed leaped to his feet with a howl of rage. 'Disappeared? What are you talking about?'

'Completely vanished, sir. The last two routing signals just haven't arrived. It could be a communications fault of course—our tracking equipment's none too good. But nothing we can do seems to raise them. There's absolutely no trace of any signal.'

'No trace? There's got to be. Sorak, you must do everything in your power to locate that ship.'

'We have already, sir, and—'

'Then do it again,' screamed Soldeed. 'That ship *must* be found!'

'Yes sir,' said Sorak woodenly. With a tinge of malice he added. 'I take it the Nimon will have to be informed?'

Soldeed looked hard at him, but he knew Sorak was right. There were responsibilities as well as privileges in being the sole channel of communication with the Nimon.

With as much dignity as he could muster, Soldeed rose and took up his staff. '*I* will inform the Nimon, Sorak. You find that ship!'

In the engine room of the Skonnan ship, Sardor and Romana looked on as the Doctor emerged from an inspection tunnel which gave access to the drive system. 'These engines of yours have seen better days haven't they, Sardor?'

'This ship was a battle cruiser of the First Skonnan Empire. It has seen long and honourable service but this is its final mission. Soon it will be replaced.'

'The sooner the better! It's a real hotch-potch, very old engines patched up with ultra-modern equipment. No wonder you're having trouble the different parts just aren't compatible.'

'Sounds just like the TARDIS,' muttered Romana.

'Can you get the engines working again?' demanded Sardor.

The Doctor ignored him. 'It's a funny thing, but I

30

could swear that the new spare parts were a product of some totally alien technology . . . '

Sardor shoved his blaster under the Doctor's nose. 'Can you make them work?'

'I don't know if you've noticed, Romana,' said the Doctor thoughtfully, 'but, somehow, people's scientific curiosity declines sharply once they start waving blasters around!'

'*Can you make them work?*' screamed Sardor.

The Doctor looked at him in mild surprise. 'Yes, of course I can make them work. The question is, can we generate sufficient power sufficiently quickly to take the ship up to escape-velocity, before we end up in a black hole over the event horizon.'

'Before what?'

'Just hold that blaster steady and don't tax your mind.'

'Do you think you can raise enough power?' asked Romana.

'Not with the antiquated drive system they're using. Just not enough *push*.'

'What about using the Hymetusite as a booster? It's an enormously rich energy source, and if we could convert the drive unit to accept it . . . '

'Romana, that is brilliant!' said the Doctor admiringly. 'I wish I'd thought of that!'

'You will, Doctor, you will!'

The Doctor waved her towards the inspection hatch. 'You'd better take a look, see what you think.' He turned to the baffled Sardor. 'Now listen, I'll need some equipment from my own ship. You'd better get a couple of Hymetusite crystals up here, ready to be linked to the energy cells.'

Sardor hesitated, looking suspiciously at the Doctor. 'How do I know I can trust you?'

'Why don't you just let me have the gun? Then I can

31

keep an eye on myself, make sure I don't get up to any funny business.'

So persuasive was the Doctor's tone that Sardor almost handed over the blaster. 'Don't play the fool with me, Doctor!'

The Doctor grinned and turned back to the inspection tunnel. 'What do you think, Romana? If we use the gravitic anomaliser from the TARDIS to counteract the gravitational pull . . .'

Romana's voice came echoing back. 'I *think* it will work. You're right though, it's a very odd mixture of technologies in here.'

'Now listen, when he brings you the Hymetusite . . .'

Romana emerged from the tunnel. 'It's all right, Doctor. I know what to do.'

'Good girl!' I'll just pop back to the TARDIS for the anomaliser.' He took out his sonic screwdriver. 'Here, you'll need this, make sure you look after it.'

'No thanks, I've made one of my own.' Romana took a very similar object from her own pocket and held it out.

'You *made* this?'

Romana nodded.

The Doctor examined the second sonic screwdriver in astonishment. He compared the two instruments, one in each hand. Romana's was both lighter and slimmer than his own, and he suspected that it was even more efficient. 'Well, quite a good try, a bit basic though.' He handed Romana a screwdriver and turned away.

'Just a moment, Doctor!' Romana held out her hand. 'You've given me back the wrong one. This is your sonic screwdriver!'

'What? Oh, so it is, terribly sorry!'

They exchanged screwdrivers and Romana went back into the tunnel. The Doctor turned to Sardor who was still covering him uncertainly with his blaster, barring the way to the door. 'Well, do you want to get your ship out of here, or don't you?'

Sardor stepped reluctantly aside.

'That's the idea! Now you go and get those crystals. Oh, and try being a bit nicer to your passengers, will you.'

'Weakling scum,' muttered Sardor automatically. They set off down the corridor and went their separate ways, the Doctor to the TARDIS, Sardor to fetch two of the lead caskets.

Back in the TARDIS, the Doctor found K9 almost drowned in a sea of his own computer readout tape. The little automaton had been hard at work.

The Doctor leaned down and patted him. 'Well, K9, how does it look?'

'Damage report complete, Master.'

'And?'

'Defense shields completely inoperative.'

'Yes, I know. Go on.'

'Dematerialisation circuits also inoperative.'

'Yes,' said the Doctor thoughtfully. 'We're right up a gum tree without a paddle, you might say.'

'Please define gum tree.'

'What? Oh, it's just a tree you get gum from.'

K9 absorbed the information and found it illogical. 'Kindly define use of missing paddle when up gum tree.'

Since the Doctor had muddled two common Earth sayings, the question was difficult to answer. 'You just don't understand Earth idioms, K9.'

'Affirmative.'

'How's the dimensional stabiliser?'

'Fused, Master.'

'Gravitic anomaliser?'

'Functioning normally.'

'Good!' The Doctor detached that particular piece of

equipment from the console. 'I'll take that with me then. By the way, K9, does the Skonnan Empire mean anything to you?'

Pleased as always to be asked for information, K9 gave a happy electronic burble and wagged his tail antenna. 'Skonnan Empire; military dictatorship extending over one hundred star systems. Collapsed from within after civil war.'

K9 went on to give a brief digest of the savage and bloody history of Skonnos.

'So those are the people we're mixed up with—a set of ruthless murderers, determined to make a comeback.'

'Define, comeback, Master.'

'That fool in there was babbling about a *second* Skonnan Empire. They've got some scheme that involves Hymetusite crystals and human sacrifice to something called the Nimon . . . ' The Doctor scratched his head. 'You know, K9, I don't like the sound of things at all! There's something very nasty indeed going on on Skonnos . . . '

4

Asteroid

By the time the Doctor got back to the engine room of the Skonnan spaceship, it was only too clear that they had been drawn dangerously close to the embryo black hole.

Gravity was so strong now that it took considerable effort to move. Even their voices sounded heavy and slurred.

Sardor had delivered the two Hymetusite crystals and Romana was already well advanced with the power unit conversion. The Doctor helped her to patch the gravitic anomaliser into the drive units.

As they emerged from the inspection tunnel there was a series of echoing clangs as meteorites large and small crashed into the ship's hull. The ship was being caught up in a stream of space debris being drawn remorselessly towards the black hole.

'It's getting worse,' said Romana.

'Never mind, we're nearly ready now.'

Sardor was hanging about irresolutely, still covering them with his blaster, though he knew by now that things were well out of his control. These two extraordinary strangers seemed to have taken over his ship.

'Now then, Captain,' said the Doctor briskly. 'I want you to go back to your flight deck and switch on the power. Keep her at minimum thrust.'

'Then what?'

'Then nothing. Just keep the engines ticking over until I come up and tell you to run up to full power.'

Sardor hestitated.

'Hurry man,' snapped the Doctor. 'Can't you feel this gravity? It'll be too late soon. And remember, wait for my signal.'

Sardor moved labriously away.

The Doctor turned to Romana. 'Sure you know what to do?'

'When he starts the engines I link the gravity anomaliser to the main circuit. What will you be doing, Doctor?'

'I'm going to patch up the TARDIS so I can move her into the hold of this ship. Then we can ride out of the gravity whirlpool inside the ship, park somewhere safe and repair the rest of the damage at our leisure.'

'Do you think you can get the TARDIS inside here?'

'Well I could—if the dimensional stabiliser was working.'

Romana looked alarmed, and the Doctor grinned. 'It's all right, K9 says its only fused. I'll fix it up in no time.'

With a cheery wave the Doctor left the hold. Fighting against the ever-increasing gravity, Romana made her way back inside the inspection tunnel and set to work.

Just as the last of her preparations were complete, the engines started up with a low whine of power. Working quickly, Romana linked in the gravity anomaliser. Almost immediately the gravity started to lessen and she could move freely again . . .

In the control room, Sardor sat hunched over the controls. The dead body of Sekkoth had been heaved out of the way and dumped unceremoniously in a corner. Rapidly Sardor checked over his instruments. As far as

36

he could see all systems were fully operational again. Slowly he began to build up the power . . .

Helped by K9, the Doctor was working rapidly on the dimensional stabiliser. If the emergency repair would hold long enough for one short spatial transition . . .

As K9 welded two circuits together with his nose-laser, the Doctor winced and snatched away his fingers. 'Careful, K9!'

'Apologies, Master.'

'That's all right,' said the Doctor generously. 'How's the gravity pull now?'

'Still increasing, Master.'

'We'd better get a move on!'

They went on with their work.

In the control room of the Skonnan battle cruiser, Sardor came to a decision. He ran the power higher, higher until it was throbbing at maximum.

Just a few more minutes . . .

His hand hovered over the main drive lever . . .

Her work completed Romana made her way to the adjoining hold where she found the Anethan captives huddled together in their usual panic. 'What's happened?' asked Seth.

'It's all right,' said Romana reassuringly. 'We'll be away from here soon. All we've got to do now is wait for the Doctor.'

'If we get away from here, we'll be taken to Skonnos. We'll still be sacrificed.'

'Then take over the ship. Once we're free of the gravity whirlpool, you can make the pilot take you home

37

again.'

Teka was horrified. 'We can't do that! We have to go to Skonnos.'

'I don't see why!'

'Because if we don't send the sacrifice,' said Seth gloomily, 'the Skonnons will send their battle fleet to destroy our planet.'

'What, with ships like this one?'

'They will send their great battle fleet,' whispered Teka. 'It is a fearsome sight.'

'Have you ever seen this fleet?'

'Our ancestors did, in the days of the first conquest. They say it blotted out the daylight.'

'Well, if the rest of their ships are in the same state as this one, you would see them off with a good shout and a few well-aimed stones!'

The Anethans stared dumbly at her.

In the control room, Sardor ran the power to maximum, threw the power lever to full and cut in the main drive.

With a sudden surge of power that rattled every hull-plate the ancient cruiser leaped into life.

Romana said, 'Well I think you're all being very feeble about—' She broke off and clutched at the bulkhead. 'We're moving. The ship's in flight and the Doctor isn't back yet. The pilot was supposed to wait!'

She ran from the hold.

The energy corridor between TARDIS and ship lengthened and snapped as the ship surged away . . . leaving the TARDIS behind, still held by the gravity whirlpool.

Fragments of space debris began bumping against the outside of the police box.

Romana dashed into the control room. 'You despicable worm! You've left the Doctor behind. Turn back at once!'

Sardor was hunched over the controls. 'My duty is to deliver my cargo to Skonnos—and we're late already.'

'Your duty is to the Doctor—he just saved your life!'

'No! I must deliver the sacrifice. The Great Contract must be fulfilled.'

Romana tried to pull him from the controls, but he shoved her away, snatching the blaster from his belt. 'Turn back,' shouted Romana. 'Please, you must turn back.'

'We go to Skonnos. The Nimon waits for no-one.'

The sudden break with the space ship set the TARDIS spinning, and once more the Doctor was thrown from his feet. He picked himself up and staggered to the console. On the scanner he could see the rapidly disappearing battle cruiser.

'He's left us, just gone off and left us. The miserable weasel! And he's taken Romana.' The Doctor shook his head. 'Poor Romana, what's going to happen to her? What's going to happen to us, come to that?'

'Master!'

'What is it, K9?'

'Large object approaching at considerable speed.'

The Doctor looked at the scanner and saw an enormous chunk of rock, growing larger and larger as it came nearer. 'Looks like some kind of asteroid. What do you make of it, K9?'

'Estimated mass equivalent to 220 million tons,'

reported K9 calmly. 'Diameter 96.4 kilometres. Now approaching at a speed of Mach 9.3.'

'That's not an asteroid,' yelled the Doctor. 'It's practically a planet—and it's heading straight towards us.'

On the screen the giant asteroid grew rapidly larger as it rushed towards them.

5

The Nimon

'The object is now on a collision course,' said K9, with his usual infuriating calm.

'How long have we got?'

'Estimated time to impact, 89.4 seconds.'

'89.4 seconds,' repeated the Doctor. 'No defence shields, no dematerialisation circuit, only half power on main drive . . . You know what, K9, I think we're going to find out what it's like to be a cricket ball!' He patted the TARDIS, 'Well, it's been a great partnership, old girl.'

'Master?'

The Doctor looked down. 'This is no time for petty jealousies, K9! You've been a good dog, the best I've ever had.'

'Thank you, Master,' said K9 primly. 'Time to impact now 58 seconds dead.'

The Doctor shuddered. 'I do wish you wouldn't use words like that! Wait a minute—did I say cricket ball?' He rushed back to the console.

Still covering Romana with his blaster, Sardor was adjusting the navigational controls with his other hand. Suddenly a steady bleep filled the cabin. 'The beacon!

We made it—we're back on course for Skonnos!'

'No!' shouted Romana. 'We've got to go back for the Doctor.' Slipping into the co-pilot's seat she began wrestling with the controls.

Sardor grabbed her by the arm and dragged her to the door. 'Come on, you, into the hold—move! For all I care you friend can rot in his black hole!'

With carefully timed bursts of power, the Doctor managed to increase the TARDIS's rate of spin until it was whirling wildly. Clinging to the console he glanced at the scanner screen, now entirely filled by the enormous asteroid. 'Brace yourself, K9, here we go!'

The asteroid struck the TARDIS with a crash that sent the Doctor and K9 flying across the control room . . . and sent the TARDIS itself whirling away through space, like a spinning cricket ball struck by some enormous bat.

The Doctor staggered giddily to the console and fought to bring the TARDIS out of its spin. Gradually he succeeded and things returned, more or less, to normal.

He shook his head, unable to rid himself for a moment of the sensation that the TARDIS was still whirling round.

'Are you all right, K9?'

K9 glided rather erratically from the far corner of the control room. 'Affirmative, Master.'

'Good,' said the Doctor weakly. 'How am I?'

K9 scanned the Doctor. 'There appears to be no damage to your circuitry.'

'That's nice to know. Let's hope the same is true of the TARDIS.' He began checking over the console. 'Well, we did it, K9!'

'Please clarify, Master. Did what?'

'I just put a whole lot of spin on the TARDIS, so that the asteroid batted us clear out of the gravity whirlpool. You know, K9, I sometimes think I'm wasting my time dashing round the cosmos saving planets from destruction. With talents like mine, I could have played cricket for England!'

Dressed in his full ceremonial regalia, his staff of office in his hand, Soldeed paced up and down in front of the Power Complex. He did not relish bringing bad news to the Nimon, but he knew there was no alternative.

Finally Soldeed nerved himself to his task. Marching up to the gleaming metal doorway he raised his staff. 'In the name of the Second Skonnan Empire!'

Soldeed stepped through the shimmering red curtain and disappeared from the sight of the awe-stricken guards.

He found himself in the same maze of featureless metal corridors that he had encountered on previous visits. They twisted away in all directions, branching off here and there, bending in odd distorted angles.

Resolutely Soldeed set off. It didn't much matter which direction he took. All paths led eventually to the centre—and the Nimon.

He marched on, taking turning after turning.

Suddenly he heard a low, rumbling roar. He was close to the abode of the Nimon.

He turned a corner and found himself in a huge circular control room, lined with strange alien machinery. Set into the far wall was a curved screen of shining metal. A great black figure was hunched over one of the consoles, dwarfing the instruments with its enormous bulk. It swung round as Soldeed entered and spoke in a deep rumbling voice. 'Why do you dare to disturb me at this time?'

As always when he looked on the face of the Nimon, Soldeed became speechless with terror.

It was a fearsome, extraordinary creature, not unlike the great buffalo of Earth. Presumably on the Nimon's planet some similar creature had developed intelligence and become the dominant life form. The Nimon was like a great black bull that had learned to talk and walk upon its hind legs like a man. The massive head merged directly into the enormous torso, with no suggestion of a neck. Great golden eyes blazed with a fierce intelligence and two amber-coloured horns jutted from the broad flat forehead. The creature wore only a wide jewelled belt and a kind of metallic kilt.

The most terrifying thing about the Nimon was that it was never still. It was as if so much energy was packed into the enormous body that it throbbed with continual power, pacing restlessly to and fro like a great caged beast. Even when it was not speaking it gave off a constant series of low, rumbling growls.

Soldeed took an instinctive pace back as the Nimon moved towards him. 'Well, Soldeed?'

In a voice shaking with fear, Soldeed told of the loss of the ship bearing the tribute.

The Nimon listened restlessly, punctuating Soldeed's rambling speech with low angry growls. 'Enough!' it roared at last. 'You dare to speak to me of failure, Soldeed? Be mindful of the terms of our Great Contract.'

'I am, Lord Nimon.'

'Be mindful of what you have undertaken to perform. The tributes *must* be brought before me. There can be no stumbling on the Great Journey of Life.'

'Indeed not, Lord Nimon. The hostages shall be found. Perhaps the Anethans have attacked the ship to rescue them!'

'And what have you done to exact vengeance for such

a deed?'

'Nothing as yet, Lord Nimon. I came straight to you as soon as I heard the news.'

'You are idle Soldeed, neglectful of your undertakings.'

With a mighty effort, Soldeed found the courage to protest. 'Lord Nimon, we have almost fulfilled our part of the Great Contract, but the condition of our ship makes it difficult for us to reach Aneth. If you were to advance us some of the technology you have promised us, the new ships, the new weapons, we could complete the agreement and claim vengeance from Aneth at the same time.'

The Nimon gave a bellow of rage. 'No, Soldeed. The terms of our contract are clear. You are buying from me the power to conquer the entire galaxy. I must be paid—and I will be paid in full!'

Soldeed was pale and shaken when he emerged from the Power Complex.

Sorak was waiting for him. 'Well, Soldeed?'

'I have spoken with the Nimon!'

'And what does the Nimon say this time?'

'He speaks of many things. He speaks of the Journey of Life . . .'

'Again? What does this Journey mean?'

Soldeed was far from certain himself. 'It is a metaphor, Sorak, a symbol . . .'

'A symbol of what?'

Soldeed decided to change the subject. 'The Nimon also spoke of you, Sorak,' he lied. 'Of the vengeance he will demand if you do not either find the missing ship of arrange for a fresh shipment of sacrifices. If the ship cannot be found, then we attack Aneth.'

'It is not possible, Soldeed. There are no more ships.'

Soldeed lowered his voice. 'We must do it, Sorak. We must! Or we shall face the wrath of the Nimon.'

Locked in the hold with her fellow captives, Romana was trying to inspire them to revolt. 'Look, there are eight of us, and only one Skonnon now. It should be easy to overpower him and seize the ship.'

'It wouldn't be any use,' said Seth dispiritedly.

'Of course it would. I can fly the ship. We could go back and find the Doctor and then take you all back home, back to your families and Aneth.'

'You don't understand,' said Teka desperately. 'It's for the sake of Aneth and our families that we must go to Skonnos. If we don't, the Skonnons will destroy the planet.' She lowered her voice. 'There's only one way we can be free, only one way our people can stop living in fear. We must defeat the Nimon.'

Seth looked uneasy. 'Quiet, Teka. No one must know of our plan.'

'What plan?' asked Romana curiously.

'Seth is going to destroy the Nimon. When it is done, he will seize the ship and take us home in triumph.'

'How will your father know it's not another Skonnon raiding party?'

'Skonnan ships are all black—like this one. We shall paint the ship white before we return.'

It seemed a pretty impractical scheme to Romana, though she was relieved to find the Anethans showing any sign of enterprise. 'What about this lot, are they part of your plan?'

Teka shook her head. 'They'd be useless, they've given up already. You can see, they're too frightened even to talk.'

Romana looked at the dispirited group. 'Well, you lot can sit and whimper if you like—I'm going to get out of here.' She reached in her pocket and then gave a little cry of alarm.

'What's the matter?' asked Seth.

'My sonic sscrewdriver. I must have left it behind in the engine room!' Angrily Romana began hammering on the locked door with her fists.

Soldeed sat gloomily in his laboratory, staring out at the two enormous horns above the Power Complex.

Somewhere in there the Nimon was waiting—and he would be growing angry.

He looked up eagerly as Sorak rushed in. 'Well, have you found another ship to go to Aneth?'

'Better than that, we've found the lost battle cruiser!'

'What?'

'It just reappeared on our scanners. They've just sent a signal. There was some kind of accident and the Captain was killed. But everything's all right, the sacrifices and the crystals are unharmed.'

'Excellent. Make preparation for the Ceremony of Sacrifice.'

'At once Soldeed!'

Soldeed looked out at the Power Complex once more, but this time his gaze was exultant. 'The Great Contract nears its completion. Skonnos shall rise again and conquer. The Nimon be praised!'

6

The Maze

Romana had abandoned her useless banging on the door, and was trying to gather some useful information from her fellow captives. 'Who is this Nimon? *What* is it?'

'The Nimon is a god,' said Teka simply. 'The great god of Skonnos. They say he's a terrible creature, with awesome powers. If we don't pay tribute to him, he will destroy us.'

'Sounds like an insecure personality to me!'

Seth took up the story. 'Apparently he lives in something called the Power Complex.'

'Very appropriate!'

'No-one who has entered the Power Complex has ever come out again. No-one but Soldeed.'

'And who's Soldeed?'

'A great scientist on Skonnos. He built the Power Complex for the Nimon.'

'Indeed Soldeed is the *only* scientist on Skonnos,' said Teka.

'That's interesting. How did that happen?'

'There was a great civil war,' said Seth. 'Only a handful of soldiers survived. When the war was over the Nimon arrived, and the Skonnons began demanding tribute from Aneth.'

Teka gripped his arm fiercely. 'But you're going to change all that—aren't you, Seth?'

Seth did his best to look determined. 'Yes, of course I am.'

One of the female captives, a dark-haired girl younger than the rest was sobbing hopelessly. Teka went across to comfort her.

Romana said, 'I admire your courage, Seth. You seem to have taken on quite a task.'

'Yes, I know.'

'You don't sound very confident. I thought you were supposed to be the great hero of Aneth?'

Seth glanced across at Teka. 'Well, I'm not a hero. I never wanted to be one!' He lowered his voice. 'Oh, I've had a few adventures, mostly because I just happened to be in the right place at the right time. I'm not even a prince really.'

'You're not?'

'I'd run away from home you see—about the only really brave thing I've ever done. They found me on the road and I was taken to the King, Teka's father. Rather than be sent back I made up this story about being a great hero, a prince from some distant land, and the King believed me! Next thing I knew, I found myself volunteering to be one of the hostages. I'm supposed to destroy the Nimon and return to Aneth in triumph!'

'You have got problems, haven't you?'

'I'll just have to do the best I can when the time comes. Please don't tell Teka any of this, she's got a lot of confidence in me. I'm her only hope.'

'Don't worry. Your secret is safe with me.'

'Do you promise?'

'Cross my hearts,' said Romana solemnly. 'Both of them.'

The door was flung open and Sardor appeared, aiming his blaster at Romana. '*You*, come with me. I need you to help land the ship. The rest of you weakling scum get into the next hold and pick up those five caskets.'

*   *   *

With Romana as unwilling co-pilot the landing went off without a hitch. Skonnon guards met them at the rubble-strewn launch pad, and they were marched through the ruined city and up to a gleaming metal edifice crowned with two enormous horns.

Outside the building waited a group of high-ranking Skonnons in ornately decorated black uniforms. They were surrounded by armed guards. At the centre of the group was a bearded white-faced man in an elaborate high-collared cloak. There was a horned staff in his hand and a jewelled circlet blazed on his forehead. 'Well, Sorak?' he boomed.

The guard captain saluted. 'Greetings, Soldeed. I have the honour to bring you the tribute of Aneth.'

Soldeed looked at the little group of captives, frowning at the sight of Romana. Then he noticed that while five of the Anethan captives were clutching lead caskets, the remaining two were empty-handed. He scowled down at the two prisoners without caskets. 'Why do you bring only five crystals? There are two missing. Where are they?'

Teka looked appealingly at Seth, who swallowed and started to speak.

Romana put a hand on his arm. 'It's all right, leave this to me.' Separating herself from the group she marched up to the astonished Soldeed. 'I can answer your questions.'

'Indeed? And who are you?'

'You can call me Romana. And who are you?'

'I am Soldeed! How dare you address me so familiarly!'

'Well, Soldeed, I've got a complaint to make about this pilot of yours.' She turned and pointed to Sardor, who was trying to make himself inconspicuous at the

51

back of the group. 'He went off and left my friend the Doctor behind—after he'd risked his life to help him.'

Soldeed looked at Sorak. 'Who is this madwoman? Where does she come from?'

Romana answered for herself. 'I've already told you, my name is Romana. I come from Gallifrey, if that means anything to you.'

'Speak again and I will have you eliminated,' thundered Soldeed. He pointed to the trembling Sardor. 'You! Tell me what happened.'

'She's a space pirate, sir,' babbled Sardor. 'She and her companion, this Doctor, attacked the ship. They killed the Captain but I managed to drive them off. I captured this one at great personal risk!'

'Go on!'

'Unfortunately our engines had been damaged in the attack and I had to stop and repair them.'

Romana was outraged. 'It's lies, all of it. We did crash into his ship, it's true, but they'd already broken down and the Captain was already dead.'

'You have been warned, woman,' roared Soldeed. 'Be silent,' He turned back to Sardor and said silkily. '*You* repaired the engines, you say? How did you manage to do this? And why are two crystals missing?'

'That's just it, sir . . . I had to adapt the engines to using Hymetusite, and I had to use two of the crystals to get us home. I thought five crystals would be better than none. We've still got all the Anethans, and the space pirate girl as well.'

'Exactly *how* did you adapt the engines to use Hymetusite?'

Sardor swallowed. 'Well , sir, I . . . ' Desperately he tried to remember what the Doctor had done. 'It was the fuel cells, sir. I adapted the fuel cells!'

'You lie!'

'No sir, truly.'

Soldeed looked scornfully at him. 'You wouldn't have the skill or the knowledge to make such an adaptation, not in a million years. Why did you deviate from the set course?'

'It wasn't my fault, sir. It was a computer malfunction!'

'Indeed,' sneered Soldeed. 'Your story changes with every second. I can be certain only of this—you have failed in your mission. You have endangered the tribute to the Nimon.' Soldeed was even more certain of something else. The Nimon was going to demand a scapegoat. Someone would have to be punished for the late arrival of the tribute and the missing crystals, and it wasn't going to be him. This fool of a pilot would fill the role very nicely. 'You know the penalty for failure. You have failed the Nimon—and the Nimon himself shall deal with you.'

Guards seized the trembling Sardor.

Soldeed raised his staff. 'In the name of the Second Skonnan Empire!'

They dragged Sardor to the arched metal doorway of the Power Complex and thrust him through the shimmering red forcefield.

'Now the rest of them,' ordered Soldeed. He pointed at Romana. 'Her too!' After all, he might as well dispose of all his problems at one go.

With Romana at their head, the terrified captives were thrust into the maze of the Nimon.

The Doctor straightened up from the TARDIS console and looked dubiously at his work. 'There we are, K9. It's a bit of a botch-up, but it's the best I can do without the gravitic anomaliser. Let's give it a try shall we?'

'Improvised by-pass circuitry liable to overload,' said K9 warningly. 'Advise minimum power.'

'Nonsense,' said the Doctor cheerfully, and operated the controls. The central column began rising and falling rapidly. 'You see, K9. She'll take half power easily.'

There was a bang and a flash, and the column shuddered to a halt.

'By-pass circuitry liable to overload,' said K9 smugly. 'Necessary to operate on drastically reduced power. Advise one quarter.'

'Oh, all right, we'll try your way.' Sulkily the Doctor set to work replacing the fused circuit.

Some time later, the Doctor said, 'Right, here we go again. After five . . . four . . . three . . . two . . . one!' He crept up the power and the central column began moving again, very slowly—but this time it went on moving.

The Doctor rubbed his hands. 'Success at last! Right, K9, let's see if we can manage to reach Skonnos and recover my gravitic anomaliser.'

'And the Mistress, Master.'

'Yes, yes, of course,' agreed the Doctor hastily. 'And Romana as well!'

In the dome-shaped council chamber of the Palace, Soldeed was giving his commanders a pep talk. He stood on the central podium facing the tiered rows of seats, occupied on this occasion by no more than a handful of ageing warriors.

Not that this bothered Soldeed. He addressed the little group as if it was an enormous military rally. 'At this very moment, gentlemen, the final tribute is being paid to the Nimon. I think you will all appreciate the irony—in providing us with this tribute, the planet Aneth has given us the power which we shall use to reconquer them. From Aneth we shall move on and build the Second Skonnan Empire.'

'Hail, Soldeed!' chorused the generals. 'Hail to the Nimon!'

'Even now we await the secrets the Nimon shall unfold to us. Secrets that will give Skonnos the most powerful weapons the galaxy has ever seen. All worlds shall shudder at the name of Skonnos. Our fire shall infest their skies. We shall rule the greatest empire the galaxy has ever seen, an empire of fire, steel and blood. Skonnos shall rule!'

'Skonnos!' shouted the generals.

Soldeed stood basking in their applause, savouring his moment of glory.

Co-pilot Sardor was moving cautiously through the metal corridors of the maze. He had just one hope of survival now—to give the Nimon his own version of events and convince him of its truth.

But it was necessary to ensure that none of his sacrifices dared to contradict him. Sardor fingered the blaster in his belt. Incredibly, the guards had forgotten to take it away from him when they thrust him into the maze. It didn't occur to him that they simply hadn't bothered.

He heard voices and footsteps, and flattened himself into an angle of the wall. At the end of the corridor, he saw Romana and the Anethan sacrifices moving through the maze.

They turned a corner and disappeared from view. Stealthily Sardor crept after them, turned the same corner and found himself facing an empty corridor that ended in a blank metal wall. The sacrifices had disappeared.

Puzzled, Sardor turned back the way he had come—and found another metal wall barring his way.

There was a turning off to his right, and he took it because there was no other way to go.

In the maze, all roads lead to the Nimon.

Romana led her terrified companions along the corridor. She was frowning in concentration. Her visual memory was exceptionally good—and there was something very odd about this maze.

There was a low, reverberating roar, and the little group came to a terrified halt.

Teka clutched Seth's arm. 'What was that?'

'It must be the Nimon!'

'Doesn't sound very happy, does he?' said Romana.

Seth looked round. 'Where is he?' These corridors all look the same.'

'Don't worry, Seth. If we don't find the Nimon, I have a feeling he'll come and find us!'

'That's what worries me!'

'How can you two joke at a time like this?' whispered Teka.

'Who's joking?' thought Seth. But he smiled reassuringly at Teka and patted her shoulder.

'Come on,' said Romana. 'We might as well keep moving.' She went to make a right turn and found that the junction had disappeared. She turned left and saw a junction just ahead.

'I'm sure there was a wall there a moment ago,' whispered Seth.

'There was,' said Romana thoughtfully.

They went on their way.

After an agonisingly slow and careful journey, the Doctor managed to reach a point just over the ruined capital of Skonnos. He kept the TARDIS hovering in space, while he studied the ruined capital on the scanner.

Carefully the Doctor examined the aerial view of the Power Complex. The twisting angular walls of the building made a strangely familiar pattern. It reminded the Doctor of something, though for the moment he couldn't think what it could be.

'Well, that seems to be the centre of everything, K9. We'd better start by taking a look at it.'

'Sensors detect hemispherical forcefields, approximate strength 7,300 megazones.'

'I see. We'll just have to land somewhere outside it, then. Somewhere inconspicuous.'

The Doctor began adjusting the controls.

Unfortunately a slight malfunction in the TARDIS's directional circuits caused it to materialise in what was the least inconspicuous spot on the whole planet—directly outside the main entrance to the Power Complex.

Grabbing his hat and scarf, he stepped out of the TARDIS—and found himself surrounded by armed guards.

7

Sardor's Bluff

The Doctor raised his hat and bowed politely. 'Good morning, gentleman. Or is it evening, here? Lovely day, isn't it? Or do I mean wasn't it?'

The guards looked at him uncertainly. The materialisation of the TARDIS had already filled them with awe and they had no idea how to deal with this strange alien figure.

Deciding that whatever was unknown must also be dangerous, they covered him with their blasters.

The Doctor sighed. 'Oh, no, not again! Why is it wherever I go in this universe there are idiots like you pointing guns or blasters or phasers at me?' He took a step forward and the guards raised their weapons threateningly. 'All right, all right,' said the Doctor hastily. 'Don't do anything rash, this is just a flying visit. Tell you what, why don't you just take me to your leader?'

'Take him to Soldeed,' ordered the guard commander.

Before very long, the Doctor was being marched into Soldeed's laboratory. The guards shoved him inside and retreated hastily.

Soldeed, as usual, was fiddling with a complex piece of equipment. He looked up in astonishment at his unexpected visitor. 'What is this? Who are you?'

'Hello, I'm the Doctor. I've just dropped in for a chat.

59

I take it you must be Soldeed?' The Doctor picked up the equipment Soldeed had been working on. 'Well, well, this is very interesting. Having a bit of trouble with the neutron conversion, I see.'

'What do you know of such matters?'

'Oh, I dabble a little you know, this and that! And you?'

Soldeed waved his arm around the cluttered laboratory. 'All that you see here is my own invention.'

'Is it indeed? Then it seems very odd you don't know what a neutron converter is! And I'll tell you something else you may not know. Someone's building a black hole on your planetary doorstep. I very nearly got stuck in it along with one of your own spacecraft. It's a very good thing I came along, otherwise that ship of yours would have been sucked in by now.'

'*You* repaired our ship?'

'That's right, with a little help from my friend Romana. You haven't seen her have you?' The Doctor held out his hand about five feet from the ground. 'A girl, about so high, always sticking her nose in things that don't concern her?'

Soldeed looked at him thoughtfully. The girl's story had been true then. He decided that he'd better not let this rather alarming stranger know that his friend has already been sacrificed. 'I have no idea what you're talking about.'

Unfortunately Sorak chose that moment to march into the laboratory, carrying the Doctor's gravitic anomaliser in his hand. 'I checked over the ship as you ordered, sir. I found this piece of alien equipment linked to the drive unit.'

Before anyone could stop him the Doctor snatched the anomaliser from Sorak's hand. 'No idea what I'm talking about, eh? What about this then? *My* gravitic anomaliser out of my TARDIS. Now where's Romana?' He advanced menacingly on Soldeed.

Soldeed leaped to his feet, snatching up his staff. 'Where she can cause no more trouble! In the maze of the Nimon where you will be soon, you meddling fool!'

As Soldeed fired, the Doctor brought up the gravitic anomaliser, using it to deflect the ray. Soldeed stared in astonishment while the Doctor turned and ran, bursting through the guards and disappearing down the corridor. 'After him, you fools,' yelled Soldeed, and the guards took up the pursuit.

The Doctor sprinted down the rubble-strewn corridors, made a couple of turns more or less at random, shot through a doorway and found himself on the podium of the council chamber, facing a group of astonished generals.

They looked up at him expectantly, and the Doctor couldn't resist obliging. 'Unaccustomed as I am to public speaking, gentlemen, let me say this—and I should like to make it perfectly clear. I stand before you, a man who is looking for just one thing—a quick way out of here. Can anyone direct me to the exit?'

The Doctor heard a pounding of feet behind him, leaped from the podium and forced his way through the astonished group. By the time the guards appeared he was disappearing through a door on the far side of the council chamber. The guards thundered in pursuit.

The Doctor ran along corridor after corridor until suddenly he saw daylight ahead of him. He dashed through an open door and found himself exactly where he had first arrived—directly outside the main entrance to the Power Complex.

The entrance was guarded as always and unfortunately most of the guards were blocking his way to the TARDIS. With a clattering of feet, Soldeed, Sorak and still some other guards appeared behind him cutting off his retreat.

There was only one way for the Doctor to go— through the shimmering red forcefield that guarded the entrance to the Power Complex. He sprinted across the little square and disappeared through the forcefield in one flying leap.

'He's gone into the Complex,' yelled Sorak. 'After him!'

Soldeed held up his hand. 'No! This is exactly as I planned. Now the Nimon will deal with him. Goodbye, Doctor!'

Shaking his head to clear away the dazzle of the forcefield the Doctor saw that he was in a strangely angled, metal corridor. There was no sign of the entrance through which he had come. Just the corridor, twisting away to left and right, with here and there a junction-point. He was in a maze.

Thoughtfully the Doctor fished through his pockets and came up with a packet of sticky-backed paper stars. He stuck one on the wall beside him, and then set off, sticking up a star every now and again to mark his route.

The stars should have stopped him from getting lost in the maze—but they didn't. Turning a corner, he came to a dead end and turned to retrace his steps.

He hadn't gone very far when he found himself facing another dead end—and the trail of paper stars was nowhere to be seen.

Scratching his head, the Doctor took the only possible turning, the one to the left, and went on his way.

Romana and her little party emerged into a long hall. There was a slab in the centre and on it lay the still body of a young Anethan. His skin was grey and lifeless and the whole body looked curiously frail. It was a hollow shell, like the body of a fly that has been drained dry by a spider.

'What happened to him?' whispered Teka. 'Is he dead?'

Romana moved forward to examine the body. 'Yes. It's as though something has sucked the life force out of him, left just a husk.'

Teka came forward in fascinated horror. 'That's what's going to happen to us. It's not just the Hymetusite that's the tribute, it's us too. The Nimon did this, didn't he?'

Romana nodded.

'Seth will kill him, won't you Seth?'

'If I can—and if he can be killed.'

'You'll destroy him, Seth. You must!'

'He'll get his chance, if we don't keep moving,' said Romana. 'Come on.'

They moved on their way.

They came out of the chamber and into another larger one, a kind of hall. Here they saw alcoves, row upon row of them lining the walls. The alcoves were empty, all except for one, in which stood an Anethan body. Its face was white and still.

Seth stared unbelievingly at this new horror. 'Is he dead?'

Romana reached out and touched the body on the cheek. It was icy cold. 'No, he seems to be in some kind of suspended animation. This must be the Nimon's deep-freeze.'

'What do you mean?'

'Well, by the look of that poor husk next door, I'd say the Nimon lives by ingesting the binding energy of organic compounds—such as flesh.' Romana looked round and saw a heavy metal door, rather like that of an oven, with dials and a control panel beside it. 'Looks like an atomic furnace—I wonder what the Nimon needs that for?'

'What do we do now?' asked Seth.

'There's no point in hanging about here. We'd better keep moving, see if we can find a way out.'

'Oh no you don't,' said a familiar voice behind them. 'You're all going to stay right here.'

It was Sardor, the co-pilot, and he was covering them with his blaster.

What do you think you're doing?' demanded Romana. 'We're all in this together now.'

'Oh no we're not. I'm going to get out of here! Now close up into a group, I want you all together in front of me.'

The Anethans closed around Romana, and Sardor gave a nod of satisfaction. 'That's better.' He raised his voice. 'Lord Nimon, do you hear me? We are here . . . I bring you the sacrifices from Aneth!'

A low thunderous roar came from somewhere close by.

Sardor raised his blaster. 'Don't move, any of you!' From behind them a deep voice rumbled. 'Who dares summon the Nimon?'

They turned—and saw the Nimon standing in the doorway.

The Anethans looked in utter terror at the black bull-like figure in it's shining harness. Several of them fell to their knees.

Romana studied the great creature with detached scientific curiosity, recognising the fierce intelligence in the blazing eyes, the immense energy stored in the enormous body. This was a formidable being.

Sardor swallowed, and managed at last to speak. 'It is I, Lord Nimon. I bring you the sacrifices.'

'I need no-one to bring the sacrifices to me. In this maze all roads lead to the Nimon.'

'They were particularly rebellious,' pleaded Sardor. I

myself brought them all the way from Aneth, they gave a great deal of trouble. Soldeed thought it best . . .'

'No!' roared the Nimon. The golden eyes seemed to bore into Sardor's brain. 'Soldeed did not send you to bring me sacrifices. He sent you to be executed.'

'No, Lord Nimon, have mercy. I brought you the tribute. Take *them* . . . and spare me!'

'You are a liar and a coward, and you shall die!'

With a scream of fear Sardor turned his blaster on the Nimon and fired, but the shots had no effect.

The Nimon lowered his head as if to charge, but it did not move. Twin beams of energy shot from its horns, transfixing Sardor who twisted and crumpled to the ground, the blaster falling from his dead hand.

The great black head of the Nimon swung round towards Romana.

8

K9 in Trouble

A cheerful voice said, 'It this a private party, or can anyone join in?'

The Doctor was standing in the doorway behind the Nimon.

Slowly the great horned head swung round to face him. The Nimon gave a low rumble of anger.

'So, you're the great Nimon, are you? Is it true that you're very, very fierce?' The Doctor looped his trailing scarf, holding it out like a matador's cape, edging around the angry Nimon in a wide circle.

Suddenly the Nimon lowered its head and the energy-rays blasted from its horns. The Doctor spun gracefully aside and the rays missed. They blasted the door from the storage compartment, and the body toppled stiffly to the ground.

The Nimon wheeled round, ready to charge again. Suddenly Romana noticed the fallen blaster. She snatched it up and fired, not at the Nimon, since she knew that would be useless, but at the control panel beside the heavy metal door of the atomic furnace. As she'd hoped, the panel exploded in flames and a cloud of dense black smoke rolled across the room, temporarily blinding the Nimon.

'Run for it, all of you!' yelled the Doctor, and shot out of the door. Romana was close behind him. Seth grabbed

Teka's arm and pulled her after them. The rest of the Anethan sacrifices were too terrified to move.

Emerging from the smoke the Nimon glared angrily at them. 'Do not move, or you will die!' It swung towards the door, as if about to pursue the fugitives, hesitated, and went over to the control panel.

Despite the amount of smoke and flame, the damage was relatively slight. The Nimon gave a low rumble of satisfaction. 'Fools! Did they think they could check the Great Journey of Life by such petty tricks? This can soon be repaired. The programme will continue!'

It swung round on the sacrifices, who stood huddled in a group, still clutching their lead caskets. 'So, you bring me a mere five crystals, do you?'

Unused to speaking for themselves, the captives instinctively looked around for their leaders. But Seth and Teka were gone. In desperation the tiny dark-haired girl babbled, 'It's not our fault, Lord Nimon. The spaceship broke down and they had to use two of the crystals to get us here.'

She was silenced by an angry bellow from the Nimon. 'Enough! Five crystals will suffice!' The Nimon slid open a locker revealing shelves crammed with tools and spare parts. Rumbling impatiently, it set to work to repair the shattered panel.

Romana stopped running and found that, although Seth and Teka were still with her, the Doctor was nowhere to be seen. Somehow they'd lost him in the ever-changing maze of metal corridors. 'Doctor!' she called. There was no reply.

'Perhaps he went a different way, with the others,' suggested Teka.

'Or else the Nimon got him,' said Seth gloomily.

Romana said impatiently, 'That's a cheerful thought!

Well, all we can do is go on looking for a way out of here. That's what the Doctor will be doing, he'll make for the TARDIS.'

They hurried on their way, though as usual the sameness of the corridors made it impossible to keep any real sense of direction. They turned into the corridor, and found themselves facing yet another dead end. 'We'll never find our way out of here,' sobbed Teka despairingly. 'I don't believe there *is* a way out!'

'There has to be.' said Romana determinedly. 'Presumably Soldeed manages to come and go.'

They heard footsteps coming towards them. 'It's the Nimon,' whispered Seth. 'Quick, Romana, give me the blaster.'

Romana shook her head. 'It's no good, it doesn't work on him. Keep still, maybe he'll pass by.'

They stood very still, waiting. The footsteps came nearer, nearer . . . and the Doctor appeared around the corner. 'Ah, there you are, thought I'd lost you. What are you doing sulking about here!'

'We're stuck in a dead end,' said Teka.

'So I see,' The Doctor looked around. 'Call this a maze? It's a cheat, they keep changing the walls!'

'Maybe they change to some sort of pattern,' said Romana. 'If we could find out what it was . . .'

The Doctor said, 'I had a look at this place from above when I first arrived. It reminded me of something, but I can't think what!'

'Shouldn't we move on?' asked Seth. 'If the Nimon does come we'll be trapped.'

'Don't worry, he'll be busy repairing his furnace for a while.'

'Why does he need a furnace? For burning the bodies?'

'No, I think he has another use for those.'

'So do I,' said Romana. 'We saw the results on the

way in.'

'So what's the furnace for!'

'Well, it's not a furnace at all, actually,' said the Doctor. 'It looked like a nuclear energy unit. Don't you think so, Romana?'

'I imagine it's fuelled by those Hymetusite crystals.'

The Doctor looked at Seth and Teka. 'Your tribute to the Nimon has a very practical purpose, you see. I'm afraid something horribly evil is being planned here. What happened to the others?'

'They were too frightened to move,' said Teka sadly. 'They must still be with the Nimon.'

The Nimon surveyed the repaired control panel and gave a low growl of satisfaction. He swung round on his captives. 'You may approach with your tribute.'

They hesitated and the Nimon bellowed, 'Would you have me destroy your planet? Approach!'

Trembling the sacrifices came forward. One by one they handed over their caskets. The Nimon slid back a hatch and thrust the glowing crystals into the fuel chamber of the energy unit. With each crystal the atomic furnace glowed brighter and its roaring increased.

The Doctor paused at the junction. 'This way, I think.'

'Surely not,' objected Romana. 'That way leads back into the Complex.'

'That's right,'

'I thought we were trying to get out?'

'Whatever gave you that idea? We're trying to get to the centre of the Complex. Actually, I suspect that the maze is set up to take us there anyway, so it doesn't much matter which way we take.'

'But why do you want to reach the centre?' asked

Seth.

'We've got to find the others, haven't we?' said Romana.

'Yes, of course,' said Seth bravely.

The Doctor marched off and Romana and the others followed him. Despite what she'd said Romana was convinced that rescuing the sacrifices wasn't the Doctor's only reason for going back. It was that insatiable curiosity again.

The Nimon made a final check. 'We have achieved operational power levels at last! The next step on the Great Journey of Life will soon be accomplished.' It turned to face the trembling captives, lowering the great horned head.

The sacrifices backed away in terror.

'Do not fear,' rumbled the Nimon. 'You shall not die—not yet.' The Nimon fired a low-intensity beam, and one by one the Anethans fell stunned to the ground.

The Doctor led his party swiftly onwards, as if quite sure of his route. Soon the maze began opening out into a series of linked chambers and Romana guessed they must be nearing the centre.

Suddenly the Doctor said, 'Aha!' He led them into a huge circular chamber lined with complex electronic equipment. 'This is more like it,' he said. 'The main control room.' He began examining the rows of instrument consoles that lined the walls.

Romana looked around. 'Quite a power house isn't it?'

'It certainly is? What do you make of it?

'Some kind of energy-transmitter?'

'Precisely! With the horns at the top serving as

71

directional antennae.'

'But what's being transmitted?'

'Energy,' said the Doctor. 'A beam of pure energy!'

'Well, of course,' said Romana impatiently. 'That's the reason for the Hymetusite and the nuclear furnace.'

'Ah, but energy for what?' said the Doctor. 'What's the ultimate purpose, eh?'

'I should think that only the Nimon knows that.'

'Well, I think it's about time we found out as well! Seth, you and Teka guard the door and keep watch for the Nimon.'

'What do we do if he comes?'

'Warn us, and run. Preferably in that order.'

'All right, Doctor. Come on, Teka.'

'Don't worry, Doctor,' said Teka reassuringly. 'If the Nimon does come, Seth will deal with him.'

Seth grabbed her hand, and pulled her over to the door.

Suddenly the Doctor put a hand to his forehead. 'Got it! Now I know what this place reminded me of when I saw it from the TARDIS.'

'A giant positronic circuit?' suggested Romana.

'Exactly. And the reason the walls of the maze keep changing is—'

'They keep switching, when the circuit is in operation.'

'Right again.'

'But we still don't know *why*.'

The Doctor surveyed the maze of equipment. 'It might be possible to work it out from these instrument readings. What we really need is a computer.'

'K9?'

'K9!' Producing his silent dog whistle, the Doctor put it to his lips and blew.

'Do you think he'll be able to find us here?'

'Certainly—well, very probably. He can follow our

72

psychospoor, can't he?'

The Doctor raised the whistle and blew again.

Soldeed, Captain Sorak and a squad of Skonnan guards were standing in a disconsolate group around the TARDIS. Under Sorak's direction, the guards had been trying to force the door. A pile of bent and twisted tools bore witness to their total lack of success.

Soldeed said wonderingly. 'It really is very old. It has the external appearance of something from a very primitive society, yet it's obviously some sort of travel capsule.'

'If only we could strip it down and dismantle it,' said Sorak longingly. 'But it resists everything we do to it.'

'Perhaps it is just as well, Sorak. We don't know what might be inside such a mysterious contraption. In any event, it seems impossible to open.'

Inside the TARDIS, K9 alerted, summoned by the Doctor's whistle. Confirming the direction of the signal, he sent out an energy impulse to operate the door control.

Soldeed gave the TARDIS door a last exasperated thump and turned away.

Suddenly Sorak shouted, 'You did it, sir!'

The TARDIS door was opening.

Soldeed and Sorak jumped back in alarm, hiding behind the TARDIS as K9 glided through the door.

'What is it?' whispered Sorak.

'It appears to be some kind of machine.'

'But it's alive!'

'Nonsense,' said Soldeed uncertainly.

73

K9 glided straight towards the Power Complex.

'Stop it! Stop it!' yelled Sorak.

A guard leaped in front of K9, blaster raised.

K9 extruded his nose laser, shot the guard down and glided on.

Soldeed jumped out from behind the TARDIS, levelled his horned staff and sent an energy ray at K9. The little automaton spun round under the sudden impact and came to a dead stop.

Astonished at his own success, Soldeed walked up to K9 and prodded him with the butt of his staff. 'As I thought. It is some form of electronic machine.' A sudden thought struck him. 'There may be more of them inside that contraption. You'd better check.'

Sorak said, 'The door has closed again, sir.'

'Very well! Take the electronic machine to my laboratory. I shall dismantle it and learn its secrets.'

Two guards picked up K9 and carried him away.

9

The Journey of the Nimon

The Doctor stood in the centre of the Nimon's control room, trying to fathom out the purpose of the complex equipment that surrounded him.

He snapped his fingers. 'I've got it!' His face fell. 'No I haven't!' He relapsed into a brooding silence.

Romana said, 'I've never seen anything quite like it.'

'For a time I thought it might be a giant matter transmitter,' said the Doctor. 'Only there's no transmat pad. But it's directional, I'm sure of that.'

'A directional beam, pumping out energy over vast distances,' said Romana. 'But why?'

The Doctor was studying the readings on one of the instrument consoles. 'Wait a minute, this looks like a bearing. Unless I miss my guess, the beam's focussed directly on the black hole!'

'*Our* black hole? The one we nearly got sucked into?'

The Doctor nodded. 'You remember I said it might be artificially created?'

'Do you think it was done from here? But why? What good is a black hole to anybody?'

'It could act as a gateway into hyperspace—with an exit somewhere else.'

'Where?'

'I don't know,' said the Doctor thoughtfully. 'Another galaxy, another universe even. But I'll tell you something interesting. When I mentioned the black hole to Soldeed, he didn't know what I was talking about.'

Romana said cheekily, 'People often don't.'

'Possibly not! But if he doesn't know about the black hole—what does he think all of this lot is *for*?'

'Power!' said Soldeed. 'Power drawn from the distant stars themselves. Power for the new generation of Skonnan battle cruisers with which we shall reconquer the galaxy. That is what the Nimon gives us!'

'Hail to the Nimon,' chorused the Skonnan generals obediently.

Soldeed was giving them another pep talk in the council chamber, doing his best to dispel the rumours raised by recent strange events.

'Each of you shall command his own fleet, and I, Soldeed, shall lead you into battle! Skonnos shall rule the heavens once again!'

'Hail, Soldeed! Hail, Skonnos!'

Soldeed basked for a moment in the applause and then waved them away. 'Go and await your orders.'

Sorak remained at Soldeed's side, watching the ancient warriors march stiffly away. 'Might I be permitted to ask a question, Soldeed?'

'You may.'

Descending from the podium they left the council chamber and began walking along the corridor that led to Soldeed's laboratory.

'Soldeed, it sometimes occurs to me to wonder exactly *why* the Nimon is doing so much for us. I mean, to put it bluntly, what's in it for him?'

Soldeed had sometimes wondered the same thing, but he pretended to be outraged. 'Do you dare to question the ways of the Nimon?'

'No, Soldeed, merely to speculate upon his motives.'

They had reached Soldeed's laboratory by now, and he led the way inside. K9 had been installed on the central workbench. 'You do not understand the Nimon, Sorak. He is as a god to us, is he not?'

'That is so.'

'It *pleases* the Nimon to be—god-like! To receive our worship, and to accept our tribute. In return he grants us—power! We want that power, Sorak. We need it. So we give him the tribute he asks. Better yet, we force Aneth to do it for us.'

'Something for nothing, in fact,' said Sorak cynically. 'That isn't natural. Perhaps that's what's making me uneasy.'

'You are overscrupulous, Sorak. One obtains what one wants by giving others what they want. If there is a little imbalance, one merely makes sure that the scales are tipped in one's own favour.'

'Can it really be that simple?'

'The Nimon *is* simple, Sorak. Brutally powerful, yes. Scientifically advanced, yes. But simple in his desires. I fawn to him—a little—and it satisfies his bestial ego. In return he will give us what we desire. I play the Nimon like a fish—on a very long line!'

Outside the Nimon control room, Teka tensed. 'Seth? I thought I heard something.'

'I can't hear anything.'

Teka relaxed. Then her shoulders slumped in despair. 'Oh, Seth, what are we going to do? You'll get us out of this place soon, won't you?'

Seth looked at her in affectionate exasperation. Teka had taken his claims to be a hero so seriously that she now had a child-like faith in his ability to deal with any problem. It was a faith that was getting increasingly hard to live up to. 'Don't worry. Teka, we'll find a way.'

77

Suddenly Teka said, 'Listen, there is something. It's coming this way!'

Seth heard heavy footsteps and the low rumbling growl that always seemed to accompany the presence of the Nimon. He pushed Teka towards the control room door. 'Go and warn the Doctor!'

'Are you going to fight the Nimon?'

What did she expect, thought Seth despairingly. Did she think he was going to strangle it with his bare hands? '*Go and warn the Doctor*!'

Teka ran into the control room.

She found the Doctor and Romana immersed in their study of the Nimon's scientific equipment.

'Something coming!' she gasped.

The Doctor looked up. 'Good old K9! That was quick!'

'No, you don't understand. It's the Nimon.'

'Come on, Doctor,' said Romana. 'We'd better get out of here.'

Seth came dashing into the room. 'The Nimon's coming. He's in the corridor now!'

Even as Seth spoke they heard another low, rumbling growl.

The Doctor looked around. There was only one exit from the room and it was too late to use that. 'Hide, all of you. Get behind the control consoles.'

Luckily most of the instrument-consoles were free-standing, so that there were gaps between them and the wall. Quickly they all found hiding places.

The Nimon came into the room.

They stood flattened against the walls in silence, like mice in the wainscotting, listening to him pacing about, growling softly to himself.

The Doctor peeped cautiously out and saw that the Nimon was going from console to console, switching on controls. Soon there was a rising hum of power.

Romana was crouched in hiding beside the Doctor. 'Careful, Doctor, he'll see you.'

'I want to see what he's doing.'

'Well? What is he doing?'

The Doctor slipped back into hiding. 'I don't know. But whatever it is, it looks as if we're too late to stop him!'

Soldeed was still boasting to the unimpressed Sorak. 'The secret of success, Sorak, is to make use of others. I use the Anethans, I use the Nimon . . .' He looked in exasperation at the motionless K9. 'I would use this creature too, if I could find out how the infernal thing worked.' He slapped K9's metal casing. 'There is power in this thing, Sorak, power! It is a staggeringly efficient piece of engineering!'

Sorak couldn't resist the chance to deflate Soldeed's pomposity. 'Surely, Soldeed, the creature can have no secrets from you, with all your scientific skills?'

'Ah, yes, my skills! Naturally they are more than adequate for the task. It is simply a question of time. There are so many demands on me . . .'

Suddenly a lurid glare lit up the room.

'Look, Soldeed!' shouted Sorak. He pointed out of the window. The horns on top of the Nimon's Power Complex were ablaze with light.

'The time has come!' cried Soldeed exultantly. 'This moment marks the beginning of the Second Skonnan Empire.' He gestured dramatically at the glowing Power Complex. 'With that power our onslaught can begin! Snatching up his staff and ceremonial circlet, Soldeed hurried from the room, Sorak close behind him.

Outside the Power Complex Skonnan guards were

milling about in terror.

'Calm yourselves,' shrieked Soldeed. 'There is nothing to fear. I shall go and speak with the Nimon!'

'Have a care, Soldeed,' warned Sorak.

'I am Soldeed, servant and advisor to the Nimon. *I* have nothing to fear!'

Soldeed marched up to the entrance and raised his staff. 'In the name of the Second Skonnan Empire!'

He stepped through the forcefield and disappeared.

The entire Power Complex seemed to be throbbing and vibrating, and the control room was lit with fierce flashes of light.

Behind a console Teka was huddling close to Seth. 'What's happening?'

'I don't know. Sssh!'

Romana peered out from behind *her* console. 'Look, Doctor!'

The Doctor popped his head out.

The metal screen on the far side of the control room was glowing, becoming transparent. As they watched, it slid aside revealing a bare metal chamber in the centre of which stood something like a giant metal egg. It was pulsing with light, and wisps of smoke still curled about it.

'A space capsule,' whispered Romana.

The Doctor nodded. 'Just arrived by the look of it.' They ducked back into hiding.

The Nimon strode across the control room and stood gazing at the capsule. Throwing back its head, the creature let out a great roar of triumph.

Suddenly a door in the front of the capsule swung open.

Two Nimon stepped out of the capsule.

The first Nimon gave another exultant bellow.

Welcome, my friends! Welcome to Skonnos. Welcome to the new home of the Nimon race, to the next step in the Great Journey of Life!'

'You have done well, my friend,' rumbled the second Nimon.

The third Nimon seemed less content. 'You are only just in time. Crinoth is finished. Without a new planet, our race will soon be starving.'

The first Nimon swung round its great head. 'Have no fear, my friend. Now that you are here, we can begin the evacuation with all speed. Come, there is much to do.' The Nimon turned and led his fellows from the control room. The Doctor and the others could hear the deep rumbling voices fading away down the corridor.

Cautiously the Doctor stepped out of hiding. 'All clear!'

The others came to join him.

The Doctor and Romana hurried over to the metal egg, studying it in fascination. 'It's a space capsule all right,' said Romana.

Seth came up beside her. 'I don't understand. It doesn't seem to have any engines.'

The Doctor chuckled. 'It doesn't need them, does it, Romana?'

'It's just as you said, Doctor. This place produces an energy beam which drew the capsule through the black hole.'

'Through two black holes,' corrected the Doctor. 'One at the beginning of the journey, and one at the end, with a hyperspatial tunnel between them. It's a sort of hyperspatial tube train! The Nimon have found a way of leapfrogging through the universe. They can travel as far as they like, more or less instantaneously.'

Teka was still trying to understand what was happening. 'I thought there was only one Nimon?'

'So did Soldeed, I imagine,' said the Doctor. 'The

81

Nimon have been clever. Fiendishly clever.'

'It's an invasion, isn't it, Doctor?' asked Seth.

'Yes, of course, happens all the time. When a race runs out of energy resources, it has to look for somewhere else to live. I imagine the Nimon consume energy at a fantastic rate, just to stay alive. They must have drained their own planet long ago.'

'And now they're coming to Skonnos?'

'That's right.'

'But Skonnos is already inhabited.'

'Only by a handful of survivors. When the Nimon arrive in force, they'll make short work of the surviving Skonnans.'

'How many more Nimon are coming?' asked Seth.

'Who knows? To make all this worthwhile, there must be thousands of them, millions maybe.'

Teka looked at the capsule. 'And they're coming two at a time?'

'As more arrive, they'll build more transmat stations,' said the Doctor impatiently. 'Don't you see? More and more Nimon, building more and more stations to bring in more and more Nimon to build more stations in turn. Before long the place will be swarming with them. We've got to stop them.'

'How?' asked Seth.

'That's a very good question! Seth, Teka—'

'I know,' said Seth resignedly. 'Back on guard again! Come on, Teka.'

As they left the control room the Doctor said, 'Romana, we're going to have to be very, very careful. There's enough power in this set-up to blow the whole planet to bits. You take a look at the capsule, I need to know everything about it. I'll have another look at the controls.'

The Doctor began fiddling with the controls and soon the hum of power started up again. The room shuddered with energy and the launch area began pulsating with light. Romana jumped back in alarm. 'I wish you wouldn't do that, Doctor!'

'It's all right, I know what I'm doing. I think I've worked out how to operate the main power control. What I want to do now is to find a way of reversing the polarity, sending the energy back to wherever the space/time tunnel starts from. Then we might be able to send the Nimon back too!'

Having studied the capsule from all sides, Romana decided there was nothing for it but to examine the interior. She climbed inside and looked around.

There was little to see. The bare metal exterior contained two enormous couches, presumably designed to support the huge bodies of the Nimon. There was some kind of instrument panel beside the door and something that looked like a locking device.

Romana was just about to climb out again when the door began sliding to and the capsule began to vibrate. 'Doctor!' she screamed, and leaped for the door, but it was too late. The door closed and Romana was enclosed in the shuddering darkness.

The Doctor was happily fiddling with the control console, when Seth dashed into the room. 'Doctor, we heard someone—' He broke off in astonishment. 'Doctor, look!'

The Doctor turned. Seth was pointing in astonishment to the landing bay. The capsule had vanished. The Doctor had succeeded rather better than he had expected.

Teka ran into the room. 'Where's Romana?'

The Doctor looked round wildly. 'She's gone! Good grief, she must have been inside the capsule when I triggered it off!'

'What are you going to do?'

'I'll have to try and bring it back again. I hope I can

83

do it in time, before she does anything silly—like getting out!'

The Doctor set to work, but in the excitement of Romana's disappearance, Seth had forgotten to deliver his warning.

Soldeed appeared in the doorway, the horned staff in his hand. In unbelieving horror he watched the Doctor tampering with the Nimon's sacred machinery. 'Get away from there!' he cried.

The Doctor went on working. 'I'm a bit busy at the moment, Soldeed, but I can explain everything—well, almost!'

'Leave that alone!' screamed Soldeed. He aimed the horned staff at the Doctor and sent out an energy blast.

The Doctor hurled himself aside, rolling across the floor. The energy ray struck the transmat control console, sending up a shower of sparks.

The Doctor looked up at it in horror. 'Romana! How am I going to get her back.'

Beside himself with rage, Soldeed raised his staff. 'Meddling fool, you shall die for this!'

He aimed the twin horns of the staff at the Doctor's prostrate body.

10

Journey to Crinoth

'Seth, help him!' screamed Teka.

Seth found that he could be a hero after all.

He hurled himself upon the astonished Soldeed and wrenched the staff from his hands. Since he had no idea how to operate it, he whirled it through the air and clubbed Soldeed to the ground.

The Doctor sprang to his feet. 'Well done, Seth! Now let's see how much damage he's done.'

Luckily the ray had struck the console only glancingly, but the surface was charred and smoking, and several circuits were blown completely.

The Doctor said, 'I don't like the look of that—I don't like it at all! He looked across at the empty transmat pad. 'Sorry, Romana!'

The vibrating stopped, the power hum died, and the space capsule door slid open.

Romana looked out. She saw an instrument-packed control room and for a moment she thought she was still in the same place. But this control room was shabby and neglected, dusty with disuse. Moreover it was deserted. The Doctor, Seth and Teka were nowhere to be seen.

Unwillingly Romana made herself admit the truth. She had completed the reverse journey through the hyperspatial tunnel. Now she was at the terminal—at the other end. Climbing out of the capsule, she crossed the control room and looked into a corridor. Again it was eerily like, and yet unlike, the place she had left behind. There were the same twisting metal corridors, but this metal was dull and tarnished, and the floors were strewn with rubble. This Power Complex, if it was one, was abandoned, its rooms and corridors in darkness.

Suddenly she heard heavy footsteps echoing through the deserted building. Two Nimon turned the corner and came marching towards her.

Romana ducked back, but not quickly enough, and the Nimon saw her.

'Stop!' bellowed the nearest. 'You! Stop!'

No use staying in the control room, she'd be trapped. Romana dashed out of the doorway and turned left, sprinting down dark corridors away from the advancing Nimon.

'Pursue her!' roared one of them, and the heavy footsteps came pounding after her.

Romana ran for her life.

The Doctor produced his sonic screwdriver and began dismantling an adjoining sub-console, looking for parts he could use to repair the wrecked main unit.

Seth and Teka watched him work. 'Is the damage very bad, Doctor?' asked Seth.

'It's pretty bad, but I may be able to fix it. If I can just cannibalise some of these other circuits . . .'

'Is there anything I can do?'

The Doctor nodded towards the unconscious Soldeed. 'Don't worry, you've done your bit. What I really need now is K9. I wonder what's keeping him?'

He hunted through his pockets for his silent dog whistle, and his fingers touched another, very familiar

86

shape. He produced a small but complex piece of equipment and put it on top of the console.

'What is it, Doctor?' asked Teka.

'The gravitic anomaliser from my TARDIS. Now why didn't I think of that before.' He began dismantling the anomaliser. 'It's an entirely different system really, but it just might be compatible.'

'Does that mean you can make all this work?' asked Teka.

'Well, if it is compatible, it'll work better than the original, on the other hand, if it *isn't* . . .'

'What?' asked Seth worriedly.

'Don't worry. There'll be a bang so big you won't even hear it.'

Seth gulped.

Suddenly there was a flurry of movement from the floor.

Soldeed had recovered consciousness some time ago and had been awaiting his opportunity. In a swirl of black robes he leaped to his feet and dashed from the control room.

'After him,' yelled the Doctor. 'He'll warn the Nimon!'

Still clutching Soldeed's staff, Seth ran from the room, Teka close behind him.

The Doctor shot a worried look after them, and then went on working. The sooner he got Romana back again the better.

Romana was faster-moving than the lumbering Nimon, but they knew the corridors far better than she did. However fast she ran, however many twists and turns she took, they always managed to reappear behind her.

She saw an arched doorway and hurried inside, hoping to find somewhere to hide so that the pursuit would pass her by.

She found herself in another strangely familiar setting. A long Chamber with a central slab, its walls lined with tiered compartments, each big enough to hold a body. The compartments were empty and there was no husk-like body on the slab. With a shudder, Romana thought that the Nimon had already drained the life from this planet. Now it was the turn of Skonnos.

She was reluctantly considering the possibility of hiding in one of the storage spaces when she realised she had left things too late.

Two Nimon appeared in the doorway.

Lowering their heads, the Nimon trained their horns on Romana's body.

She was preparing to leap aside when there was a sudden flash of light. First one and then the other of the massive black shapes twisted and fell.

Behind the fallen Nimon, Romana saw a tall gaunt figure. For a moment she thought it was Soldeed, but this man was much older. His hair and beard were grey, his black robes torn and dusty. Like Soldeed he carried a horned staff—presumably it was this which he had used to strike down the Nimon.

'Who are you?'

'My name is Sezom.'

'You seem to have saved my life.' She looked down at the two Nimon. 'Are they dead?'

'Alas no. But they will be unconscious for a while.' Leaning on his staff he hobbled up to her. 'Who are you? Why are you here, in this place of death?'

'My name is Romana, and I got here by accident. Where is here, by the way?'

'This is Crinoth—the little that is left of it. It is a dead planet now.'

'What happened?'

'The Nimon happened. They have drained the energy

88

from everything, destroyed everyone, but me.' He swayed on his feet, leaning against the table to steady himself.

Romana looked at him in concern. 'Are you all right? You look ill.'

'I am dying,' said Sezom simply. 'My time is almost up. The Nimon left me just enough energy to cling to life and see my planet die.'

Romana helped him to sit on the central slab, and he hunched forward wearily. 'You are very kind. It is more than I deserve.'

'Well, you did just save my life.'

'Perhaps, my child. But I have caused the deaths of others, so many others. I am to blame for the total destruction of my planet and of all its people.'

'You helped the Nimon to come here?'

'I worked for them, became their creature. They promised power, peace and prosperity, technology for my people.'

'Tell me, did you provide them with some sort of tribute? With sacrifices?'

Sezom looked at her in horror. 'How could you know that?'

'I've just encountered something very similar.'

'There was only one of them at first,' said Sezom brokenly. 'I swear I never knew what was to come. The lives of a few sacrifices, a little evil measured against the good of all. It seemed such a small price to pay.' Sezom began to weep. 'They are like a plague, a plague of locusts. They seem harmless at first and then they began to swarm all over the planet.' He clutched at her arm. 'It is how they survive you see, going from planet to planet, sucking each one dry and then moving to another and then another.'

Romana stood up. 'I've got to get back to Skonnos!'

'Where is that?' asked the old man feebly.

89

'Their next victim planet. It's where I've just come from.'

'You must warn them,' said Sezom feverishly.

'Easier said than done. Can you get me back to their space capsule?'

Sezon rose painfully to his feet. 'I will try. Come!'

For a time Seth was able to keep Soldeed in sight, then the flying figure shot round a corner and disappeared.

Seth hurtled round the corner and found himself facing a dead end with Soldeed nowhere in sight. The maze had performed another of its inexplicable changes.

Seth turned back to look for Teka, who should have been behind him—only to find that she had vanished too.

More concerned now about her than about Soldeed, Seth ran along the endless corridors. 'Teka,' he called. 'Teka, where are you?'

There was no reply.

Teka ran in panic through the maze, searching frantically for Seth. She saw a room ahead and ran inside, recoiling in horror as she realised that she was once again in the larder of the Nimon. Someone lay on the central slab. Moving closer, Teka saw it was Sardor, the co-pilot who had brought them to Skonnos. His body was a withered husk.

Teka backed away towards the door. Suddenly she sensed there was someone behind her. She whirled round and saw Soldeed looking down at her.

Teka turned to run—and froze in horror. The Nimon had appeared in the far doorway.

Soldeed grabbed her from behind and held her struggling as the Nimon advanced towards them.

His eyes widened in unbelieving horror, as two more Nimon appeared behind the first.

The door to Soldeed's laboratory opened stealthily and Sorak crept inside. He walked up to the central workbench and stood looking thoughtfully at the motionless K9. 'So, you have power, do you? Power that even Soldeed cannot understand . . .'

Sorak had decided that the time for Soldeed's overthrow was near. The more power he could get his hands on, the better it would be for him. If he could master the controls of this robot beast and make it serve him . . .

He began tapping K9's metal sides, looking for a control panel.

Suddenly K9's eyes lit up and his ears swivelled. The blast from the energy ray from Soldeed's staff had delivered a massive shock to all K9's circuitry. The little automaton had promptly closed himself down, going into a kind of suspended animation in order to allow his self-regenerating mechanism to go to work. Apart from shock the actual damage was minimal. Now it was fully repaired and K9 was operational again, automatically switched back to full consciousness.

He was far from pleased to find himself on a high surface in a strange room, being examined by a total stranger. K9 raised his head and his eye screens glowed angrily. 'What is this place?'

Sorak jumped back. 'You can speak!'

'Affirmative. What is this place?'

'It is the laboratory of Soldeed.'

'What am I doing here?'

'Soldeed had you brought here.'

K9 looked down. Since his abilities did not include jumping he had a particular dislike of any kind of heights. 'Kindly remove me from this raised surface.'

91

Sorak looked thoughtfully at him. Since the metal beast had reanimated, perhaps it would obey his orders. 'First give me a demonstration of your powers!'

K9 extruded his nose laser and obliged with a painful low-intensity blast. Sorak howled with pain and clutched at his shoulder.

'That was merely a warning,' announced K9. 'Kindly remove me from this surface.'

Hastily Sorak obeyed, lifting K9 in his arms and setting him down on the floor.

Sorak watched in fascination as K9 began turning in a slow circle, orientating himself with his sensors. He was in a large, half-ruined structure, only partially inhabited, with a massive energy source close by.

Suddenly K9 cocked his head, as if hearing a silent signal. 'Coming, Master,' he said, and glided rapidly through the door.

'Wait,' called Sorak. 'Where are you going?'

But K9 was gone.

The Doctor gave a last blast on his silent dog whistle for luck, put it away, and then went on with his work.

Suddenly he felt very mmuch alone. Everyone was disappearing, he thought. K9, Romana, Seth and Teka. Grumbling to himself, he finished his work, sat back, and eyed the resulting lash-up dubiously. Might as well get on with it, he thought. Either it would work or it wouldn't, and in either event his troubles would be over.

He pulled the main power lever, there was a hum of rising power, and suddenly a space capsule appeared on the pad.

Delighted by this unexpected success, the Doctor hurried over to it.

'Welcome back, Romana,' he began.

The capsule door opened to reveal two Nimon.

With a yell of dismay, the Doctor ran back to his console and operated controls feverishly.

The doors closed and the capsule vanished as suddenly as it had come.

The Doctor collapsed back against the console, mopping his brow. Now he was in a pickle. How the blazes was he going to get Romana back without importing more Nimon?

On Crinoth the capsule door opened and two very angry Nimon stepped out, bellowing with rage.

'We have not moved,' roared one of them. 'This is still Crinoth!'

A third Nimon appeared and the first two swung round on him, bellowing their complaints.

Creeping along the corridor, Romana and Sezom heard the angry voices. Moving as close as they dared they crouched just outside the door, listening to the Nimon wrangling amongst themselves.

'Something has gone wrong on Skonnos,' the first said angrily.

'The way is blocked,' growled the second.

The third Nimon seemed to be the one in authority. 'We shall prepare the final contingency plan.'

There were immediate protests from the other two Nimon. 'It is too dangerous.'

'Our people are still trapped on this planet. If it explodes too soon . . .'

'We have no choice,' said the Nimon leader implacably. 'The Great Journey of Life *must* continue—even if it means the total destruction of this planet and the death of those of us who remain!'

11

Time Bomb

From just outside the control room, Romana and Sezom watched as the three Nimon set to work at the control consoles, still arguing amongst themselves in deep growling voices.

'What do they mean,' whispered Romana. 'What is the final contingency plan?'

'There is no energy left on this planet, none at all. They must rely on the power plant on the next planet to *pull* them through. If something has gone wrong there, the only way they can escape is by converting the matter of this planet itself into pure energy.'

'Can they do that?'

'They can—but only by setting off a kind of chain reaction. They can control it for a time, but once it starts there is no way of stopping it. Eventually the reaction will run out of control and the whole planet will explode.'

'By which time presumably they'll all be gone—or most of them anyway . . . Poor Crinoth.'

'I wonder what has gone wrong on Skonnos?' said Sezom.

Romana smiled. 'In two words—the Doctor!' Briefly she explained the circumstances of her unintended journey.

'So this Doctor of yours now controls the Skonnos

terminal?'

'Well, he did when I left. I imagine he was responsible for shooting those two Nimon back here.'

Sezom tugged at his beard. 'Then perhaps you can get back after all and warn him what is happening.'

'It's not so easy as that. How will the Doctor know I'm ready to come back.'

'There is a signal device inside the capsule. If you send the signal that says a capsule is ready, perhaps he will guess it is you.'

'I've still got to get into the capsule. What about the Nimon.'

Sezom tapped his staff. 'I have this, remember.'

'So you have. I'm surprised they let you keep it.'

'It was incapable of harming them when they gave it to me—but they underestimated me. I experimented with its powers, and discovered that Jasonite boosted the powers enormously.'

For the first time Romana noticed that there was a chunk of black crystal jammed between the horns of Sezom's staff. 'I don't suppose you've got any more of that have you?'

Sezom produced another identical chunk of crystal from beneath his robes and handed it to her. 'It's an extraordinary substance found only on Crinoth. It acts as a powerful electro-magnetic booster. I've been experimenting with it for years. I used to be something of a scientist before the Nimon came.'

Romana weighed the chunk of crystal in her hand. 'Can I hang on to this.'

'Of course.'

'Thanks.' She slipped it into her pocket. 'Now how do we get past those Nimon?'

'Subterfuge, my child. Subterfuge! Here, take this. A stud near the base activates the ray. ' Handing her the staff, Sezom stepped up to the control room door and cried out in a surprisingly loud voice. 'Danger! Alarm! Alarm! The Complex is being invaded by aliens! The Nimon are in danger!'

Two of the Nimon ran towards the door, though the Nimon leader stayed at the controls.

Sezom backed away down the corridor. 'This way, this way!'

As the puzzled Nimon followed him, Romana stepped out of the shadows. Levelling the staff, she pressed the stud, blasting the two Nimon down with the energy ray that sprang from the horns.

The excitement seemed to give Sezom new strength. 'Well done! Now come!' He led her back to the control room. 'Quickly, into the capsule!'

Romana was about to hand back the staff when the Nimon at the controls swung round and saw them.

With a bellow of rage it lowered its head and blasted at them with its horns. Sezom thrust Romana aside, taking a glancing blow from the ray that sent him reeling.

Before the Nimon could fire again, Romana blasted it down.

As the great body slumped to the floor, she turned to Sezom, who was leaning weakly against the wall. 'Go, my child. The summoning control is to the left of the capsule door.'

'Come with me,' pleaded Romana.

'No . . . it is too late for me.'

There was an angry bellowing from the corridor. 'Quickly, Sezom, the Nimon are coming.'

'Hurry! Into the capsule.'

'But I can't leave you!'

'You must. It's your only chance. Give me my staff, I'll hold them back as long as I can.'

Romana handed over the staff, her eyes filled with tears. 'Thank you, Sezom.'

'Go! Go and warn Skonnos, warn everyone of the evil of the Nimon.'

Romana ran across to the launching pad and jumped inside the capsule, closing the door behind her.

She crouched in the darkness, found the signal button and jabbed furiously at it. 'Come on, Doctor. Come on!'

With a mighty effort, Sezom drew himself upright as three more Nimon ran into the control room. He shot the first down, but before he could fire again, the second lowered its head and blasted him with its horns. Sezom's frail old body caught the full force of the energy ray which flung him dead across the room.

Inside the capsule, Romana stabbed desperately at the button. 'Come on, Doctor! *Come on!*'

The Doctor paced indecisively to and fro in front of the console. Should he summon the capsule again and risk bringing more Nimon?

Suddenly he noticed a light flashing regularly on the console. A call sign, he thought. And would the Nimon use the call sign when they knew he was at the other end? It must be Romana.

He reached for the controls and the Nimon—the one they had first encountered appeared in the doorway. 'Stand back!' it roared. 'Do not touch those controls.'

'Hello,' said the Doctor hopefully. 'I was just about to bring—'

'Stand back I say!'

The Nimon lowered its head and the Doctor obeyed.

'I was just admiring your splendid control room,' said the Doctor innocently.

'Silence! Later you will be questioned, tortured and killed.'

'Well, mind you get it in the right order,' said the Doctor irrepressibly.

98

The Nimon examined the Doctor's emergency repairs. 'You have reversed the flow of the tunnel!'

'That's what I was just trying to explain—' began the Doctor.

'Silence! Did you think to prevent the Great Journey of Life by this petty sabotage?'

The light on the console was still flashing wildly. 'A capsule signal from Crinoth! I shall bring the capsule here!'

'Thank you,' said the Doctor politely.

The Nimon operated the controls.

In the control room on Crinoth, two puzzled Nimon were examining the closed capsule.

'The door is locked from the inside,' growled one.

On the floor the Nimon leader groaned, raising his great head. 'Beware! There is an alien creature in the capsule.'

'Then we shall blast it open.'

The two Nimon lowered their heads. They were about to fire when the capsule disappeared.

The transmat chamber glowed and the capsule blinked into existence. The door opened and Romana stepped out. 'I don't know what you think you're playing at Doctor, but—'

She broke off, realising that the Nimon was in the room.

'Kill her!' roared the Nimon.

He lowered his head, aiming his horns.

Suddenly a voice called, 'Doctor, I've lost Teka and—' Seth ran through the doorway, Soldeed's staff in his hand.

Immediately the Doctor and Romana ducked into

99

hiding behind the instrument consoles. Romana fished the chunk of Jasonite from her pocket and tossed it to Seth. 'Here, catch!' Automatically Seth caught the chunk of crystal in his left hand. He stood staring down at it, while the equally astonished Nimon stared at him. 'Jam it between the horns,' shouted Romana. 'Then fire the staff, there's a stud in the base! Hurry!'

Dazedly Seth fumbled with the crystal.

Recovering from its surprise, the Nimon lowered its head. Romana realised that it would kill Seth before he was ready to fire.

'Quick, Doctor,' she yelled, and jumped out from hiding.

The Doctor followed, and for a moment he and Romana ran circles around the astonished Nimon. It swung its great head to and fro in search of a target.

'Shoot, Seth,' yelled Romana. 'For goodness' sake get on with it!'

Ready at last Seth fired. The Nimon staggered back, bellowing.

Seth gave a shout of delight.

'Again!' yelled Romana. 'Shoot again!'

Seth fired again and the Nimon thudded to the floor with a crash that seemed to shake the control room.

The Doctor and Romana collapsed against the reverse consoles, gasping with relief.

The Doctor recovered first. 'Thank you, Seth, and you, Romana. Well done!'

Seth looked dazedly at the staff in his hands. 'What's happening?'

'The invasion's starting from Crinoth,' said Romana. Briefly she told them what had happened. A thought struck her. 'Doctor, the beam! Reverse it again, quickly.'

'I'll do better than that, I'll block it off altogether.' Hurrying to the power console, the Doctor removed the components of the gravitic anomaliser, stuffing them back in his pockets.

Seth looked down at the body of the Nimon. 'Is it dead?'

Romana shook her head. 'Only knocked out, I'm afraid, and there are more of them about now. It brought in two friends.'

The Doctor looked at the disassembled control panel with satisfaction. 'Well, at least we know there won't be any more coming through. And now we've got a way to deal with the ones already here . . . He beamed. 'You know, I think we're going to be all right.' There was a rumbling growl and he looked up to see the other two Nimon in the doorway. 'Oh no!'

'Look out,' shouted Romana. 'Shoot, Seth!'

Seth raised the staff, but the Nimon blasted first. The ray missed Seth, but it knocked the staff from his hands.

The Nimon lowered their heads to fire again—then both dropped, blasted down from behind.

K9 glided calmly into the room.

The Doctor let out a long breath of relief. 'Well, you took your time. I've been calling you for ages.'

'Delay in response caused by alien intervention, Master. I was stunned.'

Seth stared unbelievingly at K9. 'What is it?' He picked up the staff, pointing it warily.

'It's all right,' said Romana. 'That's K9—he's with us.'

'Listen, K9,' said the Doctor urgently. 'I want you to help me modify these controls. We ought to be able to divert the hyperspatial tunnel and send any Nimon that try to use it off in the middle of nowhere. Do you think we can do it?'

K9 revolved, scanning the control room with his sensor. 'Affirmative, Master.'

'Good, let's get on with it.'

Seth realised he'd forgotten his fellow Anethans in the

101

excitement. 'What about Teka and the others?'

The Doctor looked up. 'If the Nimon got them, there's a chance they'll be in the larder—that room with the nuclear furnace. Why don't you go and take a look. We'll meet you there when we've finished.'

'Right,' said Romana briskly. 'Come on Seth.'

They hurried away.

A few minutes later they were looking at Teka and the other Anethan sacrifices, standing still and corpse-like in the Nimon storage compartments. 'Oh, Teka,' whispered Seth.

Romana went over to the control panel and studied it. 'We'd better get them out!'

'Do not touch the sacrifices,' screeched a familiar voice.

Soldeed stepped from his hiding place in an empty compartment. After assisting in the capture of Teka, he had been thrust aside by the angry Nimon, ordered to keep out of the way until he was summoned.

His eyes blazed with anger at the sight of Romana. 'You meddling hussy! How dare you interfere with the purposes of the Nimon?'

'It's all over, Soldeed,' said Romana wearily. 'The Nimon are finished and so are you!'

'No! The Nimon will still fulfill his great promise to us! The Nimon be praised!'

'*Which* Nimon, Soldeed?' asked Romana mockingly. 'Do you realise how many of them there are?'

'Do not dare to blaspheme! There is only one Nimon. He is the god of Skonnos. He will make the Second Skonnan Empire rise again . . .'

'How many Nimon have you seen today?'

Soldeed's head dropped. 'Three. I have seen three.'

'And I've seen quite a few more. The Nimon is no

102

god. He's just one of a race of aliens come to steal your planet—and you've been helping him.'

'He said he was the only survivor of his race. He said he would make the Skonnans great again.'

'He told you exactly what you wanted to hear and you believed him.'

There was something very like madness in Soldeed's eyes by now. 'So *this* was the Great Journey of Life!'

'Face it, Soldeed! The Nimon are a race of parasitic nomads, feeding off the selfishness and gullibility of people like you!'

'My dreams of glory, of conquest—all gone,' screamed Soldeed. His eyes blazed with sudden hatred. 'You—you and your friend the Doctor! You have brought this on me!'

'You brought it upon yourself.'

Soldeed rushed to the atomic furnace, slamming the power controls to maximum. 'You shall all die for your interference!'

'Stop him,' shouted Romana. 'He'll blow us all up!'

Seth raised the staff and fired. Soldeed twisted aside and the ray missed him and struck the controls. There was a miniature explosion that flung Soldeed across the room. He raised his head and said weakly. 'Fools! You're doomed, all of you, doomed!'

He gave a cackle of mad laughter. Suddenly it cut off, and his head fell back. Soldeed was dead.

Romana ran to the controls just as the Doctor and K9 hurried in. The Doctor looked at the Anethans in the storage compartments. 'So they are here! Good, I thought they would be. Revive them will you, K9?'

'Master.' K9 glided across to the storage unit controls, extending his probe.

'Aren't they dead?' asked Seth in astonishment.

'No, of course they're not, just in suspended animation. We'll soon get them out.' He looked at the furnace

103

which was roaring loudly. 'What's all this about, Romana?'

'Soldeed threw it into overload and now the controls are fused. It's turned into an atomic time bomb, and there's nothing we can do!'

The Legend

K9 operated controls, the storage cabinets lit up, and the six dazed Anethans stepped out.

Teka stared worshipfully at Seth. 'I knew you'd save me.'

'You're not quite saved yet,' snapped the Doctor. 'We've got to get out of here before the whole place blows up. Hurry, all of you.'

The furnace roared brighter as they ran from the room. As they hurried along the corridors, Teka said, 'Have you destroyed the Nimon yet, Seth?'

'Well, in a way. With a bit of help.' He looked up at the Doctor. 'How *are* we going to get out of here, Doctor? I mean, if no-one ever managed it before . . .'

The Doctor pointed to K9 who was in the lead. 'No-one had a brilliant tracker dog like K9 before. He can follow the trail back to the entrance. On you go, boy!'

In the main control room, the stunned Nimon were recovering, milling confusedly about the room. The Nimon leader bellowed, 'The aliens have escaped us! Pursue them!'

Dazedly the Nimon clambered to their feet.

*   *   *

K9 came to a sudden halt. 'What is it?' asked the Doctor.

'Maze configuration constantly changing. It will be necessary to recompute as we proceed. Uncertainty factor very high.'

'Come on, K9', urged the Doctor. 'You can do it!'

They hurried on. At every junction K9 paused, whirred, clicked, then went on his way.

Finally he led them to a blank wall. 'This is the exit, Master.'

'What do you mean?'

'This is the exit, Master.'

The Doctor turned to Seth. 'Try raising the staff.'

Seth flourished Soldeed's staff, but nothing happened.

'In the name of the Second Skonnan Empire,' shouted the Doctor hopefully.

Still nothing.

'We're trapped,' sobbed Teka. 'Oh, Seth!'

The Doctor said, 'K9, what do you make of that wall, then? How do we get through?'

'Question not understood, Master.'

'The wall, K9. There, in front of us.'

'That is the exit, Master.'

The Doctor began to wonder if being stunned had affected K9's logic circuits. 'No, no, K9, it's a wall.'

Behind them they could hear the roaring of the furnace, and the air seemed to pulse with the heat. And there was another sound—the bellowing of angry Nimon.

'I wish you two would hurry up and get yourselves sorted out,' said Romana worriedly.

The Doctor scratched his head. Logic he thought. K9 was a computer after all, despite his dog-like appearance, and you had to talk to computers logically. They could only give the right answers if you asked the right questions.

'K9, is there a metal wall in front of us?'

106

'Negative, Master.'

The Doctor grinned. 'Right. Off you go then!'

K9 glided towards the wall—and went straight through it.

The Doctor turned to the others. 'Optical illusion, you see. You can't hypnotise a computer, so K9 didn't even see it. Off you go all of you. Just close your eyes and walk straight through.'

He urged the astonished Anethans through the wall.

They found themselves in the forecourt before the Complex. The roar of the furnace was audible even here and the place was filled with terrified Skonnons. Sorak was vainly trying to restore order.

He caught sight of the Anethans and came rushing up to them. 'This is not possible! Never have the sacrifices returned from the maze. Where is Soldeed?'

'Soldeed is dead,' said Seth.

'And the Nimon is finished,' shouted Teka. 'Seth defeated him. I told you he would. Seth is the hero of Aneth!'

'Teka,' said Seth. 'Will you please shut up?'

Teka started to cry and Seth consoled her.

The Doctor, Romana and K9 rushed out of the Complex. 'Take cover, all of you!' yelled the Doctor. 'The Complex is going to explode. Run for shelter!'

Sorak took command. 'The cellars everyone. Take cover in the cellars.'

Skonnons, Anethans, soldiers, generals and guards made a frantic dash for the cellars.

The Doctor turned to Romana and K9. 'Why don't we just pop inside the TARDIS and sit this one out?'

They went over to the TARDIS. The Doctor opened the door, ushered the others in, and followed them.

As the TARDIS doors closed, the Power Complex went up in a column of flame.

*   *   *

It was some considerable time later.

The TARDIS was peacefully parked in deep space and the Doctor was hard at work on the dismantled central column.

Romana came into the control room and looked down at him despairingly. 'Oh no, not again.'

'Well, I never did get around to finishing those modifications to the conceptual modifier,' said the Doctor apologetically.

'You don't mean you've immobilised the TARDIS again?'

'Of course. But don't worry, nothing could possibly go wrong here.'

'You said that once before, remember?'

'I've said it hundreds of times before!'

All in all, thought the Doctor, their adventure on Skonnos hadn't ended too badly. They hadn't left immediately after the explosion. First of all they'd emerged from the TARDIS to make sure their Anethan friends were safe.

They'd all survived the explosion safely and in fact there had been surprisingly few casualties—except of course for the three Nimon still in the Complex. Luckily the exploding energy unit had produced a very small and very confined explosion. It had wiped out the Power Complex completely, but there had been very little damage to the rest of the city. Since the unit had been a 'clean' one there was a minimum of harmful radiation, though the palace had to be evacuated.

Before leaving, the Doctor took Sorak aside and had a few sharp words with him about the folly of imperialist ambitions. He also had pointed out that since Aneth was both a peaceful and a prosperous planet, it was in a position to give a good deal of useful aid to the shattered Skonnos.

Wouldn't a peace treaty between Skonnos and Aneth

be an excellent idea? Much of the Skonnons' past behavior could be blamed on the Nimon after all. A very good start would be to send Seth and Teka and the other Anethans home in style.

Sorak had listened very attentively and the Doctor had hopes that he would follow much of the advice. Sorak was an ambitious man but he was practical too, without Soldeed's lunatic desire for military glory.

Romana's voice broke in on his thoughts. 'What do you think Skonnos will be like with Sorak in charge?'

'Oh, not too bad—I hope. I'm afraid the Skonnos will never be a particularly lovable race, but they've had a couple of severe lessons, first the civil war and now the Nimon. Maybe they'll learn better ways.'

Romana wasn't convinced. 'Still, I suppose they'll be too busy fending for themselves to bother anyone for a while. What about that other planet, Doctor, Crinoth? What'll happen to the Nimon there?'

The Doctor pointed to the scanner screen, which showed a scattering of planets, the solar system of Skonnos. 'Take a look for yourself.' He pointed to a distant planet. 'That's Crinoth there . . . I've been keeping a watchful eye on it.'

Suddenly the planet to which he was pointing flared up—and disappeared.

'The end of Crinoth,' said the Doctor. 'And of the Nimon too. I hate to say it about any intelligent species—but good riddance!'

'They tried to use the energy chain reaction to reach another planet,' said Romana. 'It must of got out of control just as Sezom predicted.' She brightened. 'Well, at least Seth and Teka and the others will get back to Aneth safely. It was good of you to make Sorak give them the ship.'

'It was the least he could do, under the circumstances. After the way they'd been treated . . . '

109

Romana went over to the scanner. 'They should be leaving just about now.' She adjusted controls. 'Look, Doctor, there they are!'

The Skonnan battle cruiser, now painted a gleaming white, sailed majestically through space on the way to Aneth.

The Doctor grinned. 'Poor old Seth!'

'Why poor?'

'Just think of all the legends Teka's going to build up around him. He'll have to spend the rest of his life living up to them. Terrible fate!'

'I suppose that's the way legends are made, though.'

'Yes, I suppose it is.' The Doctor smiled. 'I'm glad I remembered to get them to paint the ship white. They forgot last time, caused a terrible hoohah!'

'What are you talking about now, Doctor?'

'Oh, other places, other times, Romana. A hero called Theseus who sailed to defeat a monster called the Minotaur. It had horns and lived in a maze and demanded sacrifices.'

'Sounds very familiar!'

The Doctor said, 'You know, Romana, I sometimes think that the old legends aren't so much stories from the past as prophecies of the future . . . Still, K9 doesn't agree with me—do you, K9?'

'Negative, Master!'

The Doctor returned to his task. 'Come on, old girl, there's a good few millenia left in you yet!'

'Thank you, Doctor,' said Romana, touched by the compliment.

'Not you, Romana, I was referring to the TARDIS.'

With a sniff of indignation, Romana flounced from the control room.

For a moment the Doctor stared into space. 'Other places, other times . . . eh, K9?'

'Master?'

The Doctor smiled, patted K9 on the nose, and got on
with his work.

STAR Books are obtainable from many booksellers and newsagents. If you have any difficulty please send purchase price plus postage on the scale below to:-

> **Star Cash Sales**
> **P.O. Box 11**
> **Falmouth**
> **Cornwall**
> OR
> **Star Book Service,**
> **G.P.O. Box 29,**
> **Douglas,**
> **Isle of Man,**
> **British Isles.**

While every effort is made to keep prices low, it is sometimes necessary to increase prices at short notice. Star Books reserve the right to show new retail prices on covers which may differ from those advertised in the text or elsewhere.

Postage and Packing Rate
UK: 45p for the first book, 20p for the second book and 14p for each additional book ordered to a maximum charge of £1.63. BFPO and EIRE: 45p for the first book, 20p for the second book, 14p per copy for the next 7 books thereafter 8p per book. Overseas: 75p for the first book and 21p per copy for each additional book.